LONE STAR HEROINES

Marooned on the Pirate Coast

Melinda Rice

Illustrations by Alan McCuller

Republic of Texas Press
Plano, Texas

Library of Congress Cataloging-in-Publication Data

Rice, Melinda.
   Marooned on the Texas coast / Melinda Rice.
      p. cm. — (Lone Star heroines)
   Summary: Eleven-year-old Georgina and her family are moving to the
Texas wild frontier when their ship sinks in a storm. She finds herself alone
on the Texas coast with the fierce Karankawa natives and is later rescued
by a group of pirate Jean Lafitte's men before being reunited with her family.
   ISBN 1-55622-935-6 (pbk.)
   1. Texas early inhabitants, 1820s—Texas—Galveston—Juvenile fiction.
[1. Texas early inhabitants, 1820s—Texas—Galveston—Fiction. 2. Karankawa
Indians—Fiction. 3. Jean Lafitte—pirates—Fiction.] I. Title.

PZ7.R3647 Se 2002
[Fic]—dc21

ISBN 1-55622-935-6
10 9 8 7 6 5 4 3 2 1
0209

All inquiries for volume purchases of this book should be addressed to
Wordware Publishing, Inc., at 2320 Los Rios Boulevard, Plano, Texas 75074.
Telephone inquiries may be made by calling:
(972) 423-0090

Other books in the Lone Star Heroines series:

Secrets in the Sky
by Melinda Rice

Fire on the Hillside
by Melinda Rice

Messenger on the Battlefield
by Melinda Rice

The Lone Star Heroes series:

Comanche Peace Pipe
by Patrick Dearen

On the Pecos Trail
by Patrick Dearen

The Hidden Treasure of the Chisos
by Patrick Dearen

Retreat to Victory
by J. R. Edmondson

CHAPTER 1

· • ଅ ✄ ଓ • ·

February 1817

Georgie was cold. And wet, too, but she didn't know why. There was a roaring in her ears and her head throbbed. She was lying spread-eagle, face down.

WHAT is going on? she wondered. Where am I?

To find out, Georgie cautiously opened one eye, just a slit, and saw gray. Nothing but gray. So she squeezed the eye shut again. The roaring didn't go away. She was still damp and chilled and uncomfortable. She still didn't know where she was.

Georgie opened the other eye — just a tiny, squinty bit. Gray, gray, gray. And that roaring was still there, filling her head and blocking out any other sound. Georgie took a deep breath. Before she could change her mind, she opened both

1

eyes wide. It didn't hurt. But it didn't help, either. She did not understand what she saw.

Weak light filtered through the winter-bare branches of bushes and trees. Suddenly, a flicker grabbed her attention. Georgie followed the movement with her eyes and saw a drab bird soaring under scudding layers of clouds. Gray branches. Gray bird. Gray clouds. Nothing else moved. Wherever she was, Georgie knew she'd never been here before.

The sound, she suddenly realized, wasn't inside her head at all. It was coming from somewhere behind her. It was familiar; she knew she'd heard it somewhere before, but she could not quite place it. Roar, crash, boom! Roar, crash, boom! Roar, crash, boom!

Georgie pushed away from the ground, raising herself slowly on both hands. Then she sat up gingerly and pulled her bare legs underneath her. It was a little warmer that way. For some reason her shoes and stockings were gone, and her warm woolen cloak had disappeared, too. Strange, very strange indeed. She looked quizzically at the sand covering both hands, wondering what had happened.

She felt like she ought to know, but she couldn't quite reason it out. Her brain was moving sluggishly, like molasses in the wintertime. It was difficult to think clearly.

A cold breeze against the back of her neck jolted Georgie from her stupor. She had no idea how long she'd been sitting there, staring stupidly at her fingers. She rubbed her palms together while standing up slowly. The sand, she realized, wasn't only on her hands. She seemed to be covered with it. No, she decided, not covered — she was positively coated with the stuff, like a chicken battered and ready to be fried for Sunday supper.

And that sound! It was still roaring away behind her. What was it?

Georgie turned around. And all at once, she remembered. The memories came crashing into her head like the waves she saw rumbling onto shore.

The ocean. The ship. The terrible storm.

She stumbled toward the foamy breakers and looked frantically to the right and then the left. There seemed to be all sorts of debris washed up on the beach. Some of it must be wreckage from the *Mary Maud.* Maybe other people from the ship had washed up here, too.

"Mother!" she called.

Nothing. She tried again.

"Father! Jeff!" she yelled. "Jefferson Johnson, where are you?"

Nothing.

"Mother! Father! Captain Davis! Somebody answer me! Is anyone there? Mother? Mother!"

But the only reply was the roar of the waves, and nothing moved except the clouds and the sea.

Georgie Johnson was alone.

CHAPTER 2

She didn't know what to do. Surely someone would come looking for her. But what if there was no one to spread word of the shipwreck? What if she was the only survivor? Images of her parents and her brother, Jeff, flashed through her mind. She saw them on the deck of the *Mary Maud*, laughing and talking about their new life in the West.

The whole Johnson family had been excited about the move. They had had such high hopes. Georgie remembered when her parents had first begun talking about moving West. That's the way she always thought of it, with a capital "W." It was a special place. The way Mother and Father talked made it seem like so much more than a direction on the map. It wasn't just somewhere on the other side of the Catskills. It was the West — like the Promised Land the preacher was always talking about in his church sermons. The West — land of milk and honey.

"It is much, much better than that," Father had said when Georgie shared her little insight with him. "Far better than milk and honey, my girl. It is a place of good, rich farmland and unlimited opportunity." Georgie's mother had scolded him for blasphemy.

"Really, James, comparing Mississippi with Heaven. Shame on you!"

But her eyes crinkled at the edges as she said it, and she smiled. Mother was just as excited about moving West as he was. So were Georgie and Jeff.

On the long sea voyage from New York, they had talked about their new farm and their new life. New York, Father had said, was too crowded and the land was played out. It had been farmed too long by too many people. "But in the West, it is different!"

After much discussion, the Johnsons had decided to move to Mississippi. It was so far West that it wasn't even in the United States. It was on the wild frontier, but Father felt sure it would soon become a state. And the Johnsons would be there when it happened!

They could have traveled overland, in wagons and on barges, but Father felt such a trip would be too arduous and take too long. It would be better to go by ship, he'd said. They would sail from the great harbor at New York City, down the east coast, around Florida, and into the Gulf of Mexico to the very fringes of the United States. When they got to the mouth of the mighty Mississippi River, they would switch to a paddle wheeler and steam upstream, looking for a likely place to buy a farm.

Georgie had caught a glimpse of the so-called "Mighty Mississippi" where it emptied into the Gulf of Mexico. Captain Davis had let her look through his spyglass the last day they were at sea, the day the storm hit.

"You see there, Miss Johnson," he'd said. "There's the grandest river on the continent."

Eagerly, Georgie had looked in the direction he pointed, but she wasn't impressed. It seemed flat and brown and marshy from what she could see. But she did not say so to Captain Davis. He had sailed all over the world, so she gave him the benefit of the doubt. He must know what he was talking about. It was probably more impressive up close.

She swung the spyglass to peer west of the river and was surprised. She had expected the land to change drastically on the other side of the Mississippi River. It was, after all, the Wild, Wild West. But the ocean and the coastline curved away toward the setting sun as far as she could see, looking much the same as the land east of the river.

"What's out there, Captain Davis?" she had asked.

"Oh miss, you don't want to go that way," he'd said. "You've got Louisiana, and it's a pestilent, swampy place. Then everything west of that is owned by Spain — Texas and Mexico. They're wild, lawless places full of heathen savages, pirates, and thieves. Spaniards, too, of course."

Georgie had wondered how the Spaniards would feel about being lumped in with pirates and heathens but, once again, she didn't say so aloud. It would have been rude.

"Beggin' your pardon, miss," the captain had said then. "But you might want to get below decks. It looks like a big blow is coming, and you'll be safer down there."

"But Captain Davis, it's a lovely evening!" she had protested. The sun was a great fiery ball sinking into the waters of the gulf, out where the captain said Texas was. Georgie imagined she could hear the sun sizzle as it hit the water. The sky was orange and pink and purple. It was a glorious sunset, and she wanted to watch.

"Aye miss, pretty it is, but look there," he'd said, pointing to a speck on the horizon to the south. Georgie aimed the spyglass where he pointed and saw clouds. They seemed to be climbing up out of the water, just as the sun was sinking into it. As she watched, they got bigger, and in minutes Georgie could see them easily with unaided eyes. She felt a cool gust on her cheek.

"Nasty storm comin'," said the captain. "Get below, miss. You'll be safe there."

She had fled to the passenger compartment, but she hadn't been safe. No one had been safe. Within hours, the storm was upon them. It raged for what seemed like days, shaking the ship violently from side to side. People cried and screamed, they prayed and threw up from seasickness. A disgusting mixture of seawater and vomit sloshed across the floor as the ship lurched. The stench was overpowering. The wooden ship, which had seemed so huge to Georgie when she had first seen it, was no match for the sea or the storm. With a terrible grinding sound, the *Mary Maud* bottomed out as it was flung into too-shallow water. The storm subsided almost at once, as if stranding the *Mary Maud* had been its goal all along. As Georgie climbed to the deck with her family and some other passengers, she heard the crew muttering about bad omens.

The ship no longer floated, but the dry land was still many yards away, and the dark water between the stranded vessel and the beach was too deep to wade. The crew set to work, loading provisions, cargo, and passengers into the lifeboats so they could be ferried to the beach. But the storm wasn't done with them yet. As the sailors worked and the frightened passengers scrambled for safety, the wind howled again and rain came pelting at them from a black sky. A mighty wave wrenched the ship from where it had grounded and tossed it back into the deep sea.

Georgie was thrown overboard. She opened her mouth to scream for help but only managed to suck in seawater as the waves closed over her head. She kicked frantically and bobbed to the surface, coughing out briny water and flailing for something to hang on to. Her fingers touched something, scrabbled, and missed. A small barrel bobbed past her, headed out to sea.

Georgie went under again. When she surfaced, the *Mary Maud* was gone. The water around her teemed with things from the ship, but the mighty sailing vessel itself was nowhere to be seen. Georgie kicked toward something that looked like a crate floating in the water. It turned out to be several pieces of wood, lashed together and trailing a bit of rope. Struggling in the angry sea, Georgie managed to wrap the rope around one wrist and haul herself onto the boards. She clung there, straining to see something in the dark, until the storm finally died away. A long time later, the natural movement of the waves ushered her onto shore.

A growling in her stomach brought Georgie back to the present. She was hungry. Thirsty, too. She glanced down at her left wrist and saw a raw, red mark made by the rope. She had a vague memory of stumbling out of the surf and unwinding the wet cord before collapsing on the sand. How long ago had that been? She had no idea. And no inkling of what to do next.

Surely she wasn't the only person to survive the storm? Surely not.

Even as she shook her head, Georgie knew she had to face the terrible truth. Her family might be dead. Even if they were alive somewhere, looking for her, there was no telling when rescue might come. She was going to have to fend for herself — at least for a while.

Georgie needed food and water. Looking down at her sea-soaked dress, she realized she needed clothes, too. She had no idea what had happened to her cloak or shoes, but she wished she had them now. It was cold! Turning away from the sea, Georgie looked back toward the tree line. That would be the place to find a freshwater stream, she thought. Those trees would give her more shelter than the exposed beach, too. But she wasn't likely to find much to eat in the winter-barren woods. She turned and eyed the beach again.

It was littered with boxes and barrels and tangled heaps of wood and rope — all that was left of the *Mary Maud*. Surely she could find something useful among the wreckage. The ship had been carrying food and water for the crew and passengers.

What to do? Woods or beach? Woods or beach? She couldn't decide.

Finally, she opted to search among the wreckage strewn along the shore. It would be easier than tramping through the woods and would keep her where rescuers could see her. With one last glance at the horizon, Georgie set off. First she came to a great wooden crate, so big it came up to her shoulders. She rapped on its side with her knuckles. Hollow. Walking around the big wooden box, she saw that one side was gone. It was empty. Georgie kept walking. Next she found a long piece of rope.

This might come in handy, she thought, stooping to pick it up. She coiled it as she walked, keeping her cold bare feet just out of reach of the waves. Next she came across a smashed barrel. Then another box, much smaller than the first but, like it, broken and empty. Every so often she passed a jumbled heap of boards and timbers, some tangled with rope, some with nails still protruding from them. Those would come in handy for building a shelter, she knew, but she did not take them with her. She knew where they were, and she could always come back and get them later.

What she really wanted now was food and water. Georgie was very thirsty. She began eyeing the waves. The sea was water, right? Saltwater, but water. After a few more minutes Georgie could think of nothing else. Water, water, water. Dropping her rope, she dashed into the surf, sank to her knees in the frigid waves and, scooping up two big handfuls of seawater, swallowed them down. The cold brought her to her senses. She staggered out of the waves as her stomach twisted. She bent over and retched up all the briny water, then started crying. She was thirstier than ever.

As Georgie swiped at her tears, she saw something from the corner of her eye. It looked like . . . it was! A trunk! It was a trunk! Surely there'd be something useful to her there. Sometimes people packed food in their luggage. She picked up the rope she had dropped, then hurried across the damp sand. There had been many such trunks aboard the *Mary Maud*. The Johnsons had owned several. Georgie pushed those thoughts away. She wouldn't think of her family now.

The trunk lay on its side, spilling its contents onto the beach. Clothes! Men's trousers and coats, several fine dresses and petticoats to go with them, stockings, a warm woolen cloak, and several sets of clothes for a boy. There was a quilt, too. The bright colors of its patchwork peeped from beneath the tumbled clothing. Georgie dug through the trunk, tossing aside broken crockery, a darning needle, two soggy books, and the shattered remains of what might have been a lamp. At the very bottom of the trunk were two parcels. Unwrapping the smaller of the two, Georgie found a brooch with tiny purple stones around its edges. Amethysts. Beautiful — but totally useless to her under the circumstances. Still, the pretty bauble made Georgie feel better. She dropped it into the pocket of her grimy dress. Then she reached for the other bundle. Before she finished unwrapping it, she knew what it was and started grinning. This would come in very handy, indeed. A knife! Its keen blade glinted dully in the fading light as Georgie pulled off the last of its wrappings.

She looked up and realized the sun was going down. She could see it, a dim disc behind the clouds, sinking over the horizon. That way must be west. A whole day was gone. Now what? She had found no food or water. It was time to look in the woods. She'd be out of the wind there, at least. And though she had nothing to eat or drink, at least she had warmer — cleaner! — clothing.

The trunk was too heavy for Georgie to drag with her, so she sorted through the tangle of material. Some of the clothes were practically dry! But there was a problem. All the dresses were too big for her. They were for a grown-up lady. Finally Georgie chose a pair of boy's trousers and a matching shirt, three pairs of stockings, and a short coat such as a man would wear to church. It was so long on Georgie that the hem very nearly brushed her ankles. She bundled it all into the cloak, added the knife to the pile, then tied it up with the rope and slung the bundle over her shoulder. Last of all, she drew the quilt from the trunk and wrapped it around her shoulders.

With one last glance up and down the beach, Georgie turned away from the trunk and headed toward the trees.

She kept her fingers crossed, hoping to find a freshwater stream. But she was disappointed. Still no water. She walked along the edge of the woods for a few hundred feet in each direction but found nothing — at least not anything she could eat or drink.

By now it was fully dark and Georgie was afraid of getting lost — fearful of what she might stumble across in the dark woods and even more afraid of what might find her. Keeping in sight of the ocean, she tramped back and forth until she was exhausted. Finally she stopped and dropped her bundle. It was just no use. She was thirstier than ever.

At least I can change into clean clothes, she thought.

Her dress had dried, but it was stiff from her dunking in the sea. And it itched. Georgie stepped behind a spindly bush and looked over each shoulder. Then she laughed. Who was going to see her out here? She stripped off the dress and flung it over the bush. The wind on her bare skin made her shiver. Georgie quickly dug through the bundle and pulled out the shirt and trousers. She put them on, added the man's coat on top, and wrapped herself in the cloak. On top of it all, she wrapped the quilt. Then she settled onto the ground at the base of a nearby tree and pulled two pairs of stockings on her feet. The other pair she put on her hands. She wasn't exactly toasty, but she was warmer than she had been all day. It felt good.

She dozed off, but the cold plagued her and strange rustlings in the underbrush frightened her. Overhead, the tree branches clicked in the wind. An owl hooted. Somewhere, far away, a wolf howled. Georgie shivered, but not from the cold. She was scared and kept imagining that night creatures were creeping up behind her.

Feeling the strong trunk of the tree at her back, Georgie was comforted. But then she heard noises in the woods to her left and right and became convinced that all manner of nasty things were sneaking up on her from those directions — wolves, ghosts, bears. Did they even have bears in this wild and spooky place? She didn't know.

By the time the sky began to lighten in the east, Georgie was cramped and bleary-eyed and still so very thirsty.

· • ⚘ ✂ ⚘ • ·

CHAPTER 4

Georgie knew she had to have water, and soon, or she wasn't going to survive. She hadn't had any luck on the shore yesterday, so today she would comb the woods for a stream. She'd had plenty of time during the night to work out a plan.

First, she took the knife she'd found in the trunk, rewrapped it carefully, and tucked it into the waistband of her trousers at the small of her back. The pants were too big, so she'd had to knot two of the stockings together to use as a belt. The other pairs of stockings she rolled up and stuffed in a trouser pocket along with the amethyst brooch. She took her old dress, torn and dirty as it was, and rolled it with the cloak into the blanket, then slung the whole bundle over her left shoulder.

Starting from the tree she had slept under, Georgie faced into the rising sun and took one hundred steps. She turned left, away from the ocean, and took another one hundred steps straight back into the woods. She repeated the process two more times — left turn and walk one hundred paces — and found herself back where she started, just as she had planned. Georgie had walked in a big square, stopping frequently to listen for the trickle of running water. She hadn't found any yet, but she felt sure she would if she kept moving down the beach and repeating the process: take one hundred steps, turn left; a hundred steps, turn left.

Each time she completed a square, Georgie trudged down the tree line and tried again. The walking kept her warm, but branches constantly snagged her clothes, grabbed at the blanket bundle, and scratched her exposed skin.

And with every step, her thirst got worse. She had no idea how long she'd been searching when a sound caught her attention — a trickling, rippling sound.

Water! At last, water!

But where was it? She stood still, right where she was, barely daring to breathe, listening as hard as she could. Where was the sound coming from? Georgie turned slowly in a circle trying to pinpoint it and took several steps, but the sound faded. So she turned and walked slowly in the opposite direction. This time the sound got louder. And louder. She moved faster... and faster... and faster. The farther she went, the louder the sound. By now she was running, heedless of the branches that slapped at her face and tore her clothes. She was running so fast that she almost splashed right through the little stream. Instead, she stood in the middle of it, panting while the cold water swirled around her ankles. The waterway was small — she could cross it in two steps — but it was enough. She waded back to the bank, dropped to her knees, and thrust her face into the creek.

Georgie drank deeply. Mmmmmmmmmm. Water had never tasted so good. She gulped, swallowing great mouthfuls until her face became numb from the running water and her stomach rebelled. She retched up half the water she had swallowed. Georgie lay panting on the ground beside the stream, waiting for the nausea to subside. When it did, she cautiously took another sip from the creek, then another. Finally she stood up and followed the little waterway as it meandered through the woods.

It seemed to be running parallel to the coast. And though she couldn't see the ocean, she could hear its constant booming, so she wasn't afraid of getting lost. Georgie certainly wasn't going to risk losing sight of the stream. Wherever it went, that's where she would go. She paused frequently to slake her thirst, being careful not to drink too much and make herself sick again.

Finally, after what seemed like hours, Georgie began catching glimpses of the ocean through the trees. The stream ran near a little headland before cutting straight back into the woods. Georgie stopped. This would be a good place to build a shelter. The land here was high enough to give her a good view of the surrounding land and sea, and the trees would provide shelter from the wind. For now, she was home — or would be, once she had built it.

CHAPTER 5

It took several hours to drag enough timber from the beach to make a shelter. She had planned to use one of the crates from the shipwreck but quickly found she was not strong enough to lug one all the way to the little headland. Instead, she found shattered timbers and other pieces of wood, bits of rope, and a piece of sail. Her first few attempts collapsed — one while she was inside trying to brace the back wall with a waterlogged board. For a while, Georgie despaired. But as she sat there among the trees, she had an idea. Working steadily, she was able to fashion a crude lean-to by using her timbers to fill in the spaces between three trees that were very close together. Their trunks were actually part of the walls in her new home. She left a small space for a doorway then draped the canvas over the top and tied it to the tree trunks, leaving enough hanging down in front to make a door flap.

By the time she finished, the sun was going down. A growl from her stomach reminded Georgie that she was famished. She really did feel like she could eat a horse — tail, hooves, and all! But she hadn't found any food, horse or otherwise, and at that moment she lacked the energy to keep looking. Instead, she took a long drink from the stream and settled into her new home.

Georgie sat with her back against a tree just outside the door flap, listening to the waves and gazing at the moon rays on the ocean. How she wished she could step onto the moonbeams and follow them to her family. She smiled, remembering all the times she and her brother had slipped out of their house back in New York to sit behind the barn and wait for the moon to peep over the hills and into the little valley where they lived.

"That is the very same moon that has been there since the dawn of time," Jeff would say. "Who else do you suppose has seen it?"

Georgie would always reply with the name of some great ruler or an explorer: Queen Elizabeth, Marco Polo, Sir Walter Raleigh. Then Jeff would mention a scientist: Isaac Newton, Galileo, Benjamin Franklin. They would go on like that, wracking their brains for the names of famous people and trying to top each other. But they always ended with the same two fellows, Thomas Jefferson and George Washington.

Jeff and Georgie had been named after those two American presidents: Jefferson William Johnson and Georgina Jane Johnson. That had been their father's idea. He had fought in the American Revolution, though he had only been in his teens at the time. He was proud of his service to the country. He was proud to be an American, and he always said there was no better way to show his patriotism than naming his children after his presidents. "Look toward the future, but remember your past," he always said.

Jeff was eleven, just one year older than Georgie, and he was her best friend. They shared chores and roamed the fields and woods around their house together. They studied together, too — Georgie was much better at math than Jeff, and he always needed her help. Their mother always said they were so much alike they might as well be twins.

Not long before they sailed for their new home in the West, Georgie and Jeff had even suffered through scarlet fever together. But Georgie had been much sicker than Jeff. He recovered quickly, while her temperature went higher and higher. He had refused to leave her side. Every time she'd opened her eyes, Jeff was right there. He held her hand and gave her sips of water and made sure there was always a cool cloth on her forehead. But nothing helped. Georgie got worse and worse. Her temperature finally soared so high that all her hair fell out. Her parents thought she would die for sure, but the fever broke soon after, and she finally began to get well. Jeff was her constant companion. He told her jokes and stories, gave her an arrowhead he found on the way home from school, and helped her catch up with her schoolwork and chores. It was he who told her that her hair had fallen out. At the time, she was so relieved to be finished with the fever that the baldness didn't seem to matter.

But one day, Jeff had found her crying behind the barn.

"Georgie Porgie, what's wrong?" he'd asked.

"M-m-m-m-y hair!" she had sobbed. "My hair! I want my hair back! I don't want to be bald!" She'd caught sight of herself in the well that day as she was drawing water.

"But Georgie, it'll grow back! It's already growing back," he'd said. And it was true. A soft blonde fuzz covered her head. But Georgie was not comforted. She just cried harder with her fuzzy head in her hands. She expected Jeff to say something to make her feel better, but when she looked up, her brother was gone.

The next time she saw him, she cried again — but this time they were tears of mirth, and she was laughing instead of sobbing. She had laughed so hard she got the hiccups.

"Do I look as silly as you do?" she had asked him.

"Nope, sillier," he'd replied.

Jeff had gotten Mother's sewing scissors and Father's straight razor and made himself as bald as Georgie.

Remembering those times made Georgie smile. She ran a hand from her forehead back to the nape of her neck. Her hair had grown out an inch or so since then. With her short curly locks and borrowed boy's attire, Georgie imagined she looked more like Jeff than ever.

Somehow she just knew he was still alive. She'd know if he wasn't. Jeff was out there somewhere, alive — he and Mother and Father. And they were looking for her. She knew it, and no amount of common sense would change her mind. If she could survive the storm, they could, too. And someday, she knew, they would all find each other again.

Feeling better than she had since first waking up in this desolate place, Georgie crawled inside the lean-to, curled up in the blanket, and drifted off to sleep, listening to the waves and thinking about her family.

CHAPTER 6

· • ∽ ✄ ∾ • ·

Georgie woke up hungry. By her reckoning, she had last eaten aboard the *Mary Maud* more than three days ago. She had to find something to fill her belly, and soon, but what? It was February so nothing was growing — at least nothing she could eat. There seemed to be a lot of birds around, but she had no way to catch them. Some people snared birds, she knew, but she did not know how to do that. Father had always shot the ducks and geese they ate. There would be eggs once spring came, but it was too early for the birds to be laying now. So eggs were out, too. Fish, though, was a different matter. Georgie figured she could make a fish trap like the ones they had used back in New York. She had helped Father build them often enough. There were bound to be fish in the stream — the ocean, too — all year round. The more she thought about it, the more Georgie liked the idea of making a fish trap. She was certain she could build one with scraps from the shipwreck.

There was still a chance, too, that she would find some of the food supplies from the *Mary Maud* washed up on shore. The best option for today, it seemed, was to head for the beach.

Georgie crawled out of the lean-to, stretched, and made her way to the stream for a drink. It looked like it was going to be a pretty day. A few lacy clouds dotted a bright blue sky. There was very little wind. It was still cold, but the glaring sun made it at least *seem* warmer than it had been yesterday. Regardless of the actual temperature, the sunshine cheered her spirits a great deal. After taking a long, satisfying slurp from the stream, she made a face at her rippled reflection and laughed at her own silliness. It felt good to laugh. Georgie started humming as she picked her way toward the beach.

As she turned, a slight movement caught her attention. She could almost believe she imagined it. But no, there it was again. A slight movement under the leaves to her left. This time she heard a faint scratching noise as the dead leaves rubbed against each other. Cautiously, she approached. And the motion stopped. So Georgie stopped, too, and stood very, very still. But she was ready. And when the leaves rattled again, she pounced! Her hands closed over something smooth and round, like a stone.

"But stones don't move on their own," she said aloud. This thing did. A quick glance told her she had caught a good-sized turtle. The frightened creature had retracted its legs and head. She lifted it to eye level and peered into the hole that was front-and-center in the greenish-brown shell. Twisting it this way and that, she could just make out one unblinking yellow eye. It seemed to be glaring at her.

People ate turtles, Georgie knew. She herself had eaten turtle soup more than once. Her mouth watered and her stomach
rumbled at the thought. But then she remembered that she had
no fire. No way to make one, either. She supposed she could pry
the turtle's shell open with the knife or crack it open with a rock.
But the thought of eating raw turtle made her grimace. Yuck!

The turtle, she was certain, would be as appalled at the
thought as she was. Georgie sighed and placed the little reptile
back among the leaves. She wasn't that hungry. Not yet.

If the turtle was grateful to regain its freedom, it gave no
sign. Georgie glanced at it one last time. "Well, Master
Poke-a-long, be off with you," she said. The turtle didn't move.

Continuing on the path to the beach, Georgie began humming again and tried to come up with a plan. She had no idea
where she was or how long it might be before someone started
searching for her. And how would the rescuers find her
anyway?

"Should I stay here and wait to be rescued?" she asked a gull
hovering nearby. It squawked at her.

"Well, seeing as how you want me off your beach so badly,
what do you suggest I do?" she asked the noisy bird.

She kept talking as if she and the gull were carrying on a
conversation.

"I can't fly like you, but I suppose I could start walking," she
said. "If I head toward the setting sun, I'll be going west —
toward Texas and Mexico. Now, what did Captain Davis say
about them?"

It took a few minutes to retrieve the memory. That last day
on the *Mary Maud*, right before the storm hit, the captain had
told her Texas and Mexico belonged to Spain, and they were
wild and dangerous places full of savages and outlaws.

"Of course, I might already be in Texas, or even Mexico. I don't know where the storm left me. On the other hand, walking east along the beach will take me back toward the United States."

That was definitely an option. But she had no idea how far she would have to go to reach the nearest settlement. And what if she couldn't find fresh water along the way? At least here she had water and a shelter. After all that had happened in the last few days, Georgie was reluctant to leave her little stream and the lean-to.

"Surely someone will come looking for me soon," she said to the gull, which squawked again and soared off over the waves.

Georgie was still mulling her options when she saw the box near the water's edge. She knew immediately what it held — or once had held. Hardtack! Yes! Hardtack!! She'd hated the stuff aboard ship — dry, tough unleavened bread that, often as not, had mold growing on it. Now her mouth watered at the mere thought of it — moldy or no.

"Oh, please let it be full. Please let it be full," she prayed, remembering all the smashed and empty boxes that littered the beach.

Georgie ran down the beach. But when she got to the box, she stopped, reluctant to open it. As long as she didn't open it, she could pretend it was full. Full, full, full. And she could eat till she burst. If it was empty, she knew she'd cry. So for a long time she just stood there looking at the little wooden container.

"This is silly," she said.

Georgie dropped to her knees in the damp sand, pulled out her knife, took a deep breath, and slid the tip of the knife under the top of the lid. She had to bear down on the knife and put her weight on the handle. With a low screech, the nails pulled out of the wet wood. Georgie held her breath and pulled the lid all the way off.

The box was whole! And it was full!! Full to the top!

Georgie grabbed a piece of the hardtack and gobbled it, then started munching on another. It was horrible... and she loved it. She was tempted to eat as much as she could hold. But this was the only food she had. It would have to last for a while. She ate one more piece, sitting there in the sand, then gathered her shirttail like an apron and piled as much of the hardtack in it as she could carry. It took five trips back to her shelter to empty the crate. When she was done, the sun was almost directly over-head. It was noon. She was tired from all that tramping back and forth, so she sank down and rested against a tree outside her lean-to.

As she sat there, it occurred to Georgie that she had no way of signaling any rescuers who might show up in a boat. Since she had no fire and no way to make one, she would have to fig-ure out something else. But what? What did she have here on shore that someone would be able to spot from the sea?

Of course — a banner, a flag! That was just the thing. She would tie something from the top of a tree, something bright and attention getting.

She went into the shelter and dug through the clothes she'd found the first day here. Everything except the shirts and quilt were dark and wouldn't show up well. Besides, she needed those things. Then she remembered her dress, the one she'd been wearing when the *Mary Maud* sank. It was a bright, bright yellow. Father had always said she looked like "a little ray of sunshine" in it. Her rescuers would have to be blind to miss it. The garment was torn and dirty, but the color still showed bright through the grime.

Now, to find the right tree. It had to be tall, but not so tall that she couldn't climb it.

There, a few feet away — right on the tip of the little spit of land where she'd built the shelter — was the very thing. It stood straight and tall, with a deep fork where the main trunk split into two big branches. Draping the dress around her neck, Georgie stepped up into the deep vee where the trunk forked. Moving slowly to keep her balance, she inched her way up the tree moving one foot, then a hand, the other foot, and the other hand.

The rough bark scratched her palms and the tender bottoms of her bare feet, but she kept going. Her rescue depended on it. When she could safely go no higher, Georgie took the dress, reached over her head, and tied the garment by its long sleeves to a branch as high as she could reach. There was no wind and the dress hung limply, but its cheery color stood out like a beacon against the dark bark.

From where she stood, balanced precariously high in the tree, Georgie could see for miles and miles in every direction. In front of her, the ocean stretched away to the horizon — brown near the shore, a greenish blue farther out. She hoped to see a ship coming to her rescue, but no such luck. The water was flat and calm and utterly empty. The shore and the woods stretched away on either side, looking much the same to the east and west. Flotsam and jetsam littered the beach in both directions — wreckage from the *Mary Maud,* no doubt. Georgie wrapped one arm around the tree trunk and risked a glance behind her. Trees, trees, and more trees. Georgie couldn't see another living thing. She had never felt so alone.

CHAPTER 7

Over the next several weeks, Georgie developed a routine. At night she hunkered down in her shelter, wrapped in the quilt. She was getting used to her new home. The night noises didn't even scare her anymore — most of the time anyway.

During the day she scoured the beach to look for food and other useful things from the shipwreck. She found many boxes and barrels. Some were empty, but others contained things like nails and flour. She was able to use the nails, with a rock for a hammer, to reinforce her shelter using scraps of wood that washed ashore. The flour, however, was ruined. Seawater had leaked into the barrel and made a pasty mess of it.

Among Georgie's treasures was a silver pitcher she found rocking in the surf early one morning. It was dented in several places but worked just fine for getting water from the stream. That same day she found a man's boot.

"What I want with a single boot, I don't know," Georgie said. She had gotten into the habit of talking to herself. "But it might come in handy. I better keep it."

She took it back to her little home and piled it in a corner with the other things she'd gathered: a pair of spectacles, a bridle, a comb such as a lady might wear in her hair, a buttonhook, a length of lace, and the amethyst brooch she'd found in the trunk that first day.

Several days after finding the hardtack, Georgie decided to get the rest of the clothes from the trunk, figuring they might be useful in some way. But search as she might, she could find no trace of it. The thing had just disappeared. She looked and looked, but it was gone. Befuddled, she sat down in the sand to watch the waves and mull this mystery. Had someone come to retrieve the trunk? Had she missed the rescuers?

At her feet she noticed a strip of what looked like dead grass mixed with shells and bits of wood. It ran in a wavering line up and down the beach. Another mystery. It must have washed ashore, just like the trunk and other stuff from the shipwreck, but the waves did not reach that high on the beach. So how did the line get so far away from the water?

Of course!

"Why didn't I think of this before?" she said.

It was the tide. Captain Davis had told her all about the tides when she was aboard the *Mary Maud*. When the tide came in, it brought the trunk with it. And when it went out, the trunk went out, too. How silly that she hadn't thought of it before!

After that, Georgie learned to safeguard what she found along the beach. If she wanted it and couldn't get it to her shelter, she pulled it high up the beach into the dry sand above the tide line. One very memorable day, she found a half-full barrel of salt pork. Before, she had loathed the stuff. It was worse than hardtack. But by the time she found the barrel, Georgie was far past such pickiness. She relished the fatty meat, knowing it might be the only food she had for a very long time. Every day she ate a little bit of the salt pork and half a piece of hardtack, trying to make them last as long as possible. But she drank as much water as she could hold. She never got over being hungry, but she did learn to ignore her belly's grumblings.

As time passed, fewer items washed onto shore and Georgie spent more time exploring the woods. "Maybe there are people living nearby," she said. "If so, I better quit talking to myself or they'll think I'm crazy!"

One afternoon, as she tramped through the woods, she discovered something that made her very happy. Green. Some of the trees had tiny green buds on their branches. That meant that spring was on its way.

"Yahoo!" screamed Georgie. "Yahoo! Yahoo! Yahoo!"

She wondered if that counted as talking to herself — then decided she did not care, not a whit.

"Yahoo!" she yelled again. Then grinned.

From that day on, the signs of spring came hard and fast. Many of the trees erupted in blossoms — white or pink or yellow. The nights were no longer so cold and the days were often bright and sunny. Many times Georgie did not need her coat and it stayed in a heap on the floor of the shelter. Green spears started shooting up among the beach grass and in the woods. And birds showed up in ever-increasing numbers. So many birds. All kinds of birds. Georgie had never seen so many different types of birds in one place at one time. Sometimes she spent hours sitting and watching them. There were the gulls, of course, and great squawking black birds. Tiny, blunt-beaked twittering creatures. Ducks and jays and cardinals and robins — and many more types that she could not identify.

Georgie gloried in the changing of the seasons, but the storms it brought terrified her.

The clouds would mound up, getting darker and darker. Sometimes there would be a far-off rumble. Then, boom! The thunder would come. And lightning would follow. Flash! Then the rain came. Pitter-patter. Pitter-patter. Pitter-patter. Pitter-patter. Whoosh!

Boom! Crack! Flash! Boom! Crack! Flash! Boom! Crack! Flash! Boom! Boom! Boom! It seemed the sky must shatter under such an assault.

The pitter-patter would turn into a torrent, the wind howled, and Georgie cowered in her lean-to, or among the trees if she was out when a storm swept in. Then, as quickly as it came, the storm would race off, leaving the air fresh and the ground sodden. The days following such storms were always glorious.

After one particularly nasty "thunderbumper" — as she'd started calling them — Georgie decided to follow her little stream to see where it might lead. But this time she would not turn back when night fell. This time she would keep going. The creek might lead her to a settlement. People always settled where they could get fresh water.

She fashioned a little pack of sorts from a scrap of sail. Into it she stuffed several pieces of hardtack and some salt pork, a rag, a pair of socks, and the knife. Everything else she left in her shelter, even the quilt. It had gotten so warm that she did not need it. Before setting off she climbed the tree where her beacon dress was hanging. It was more tattered than ever now, thanks to the violent storms, but the color was still bright and attention getting. Shading her eyes with one hand, Georgie gazed out to sea, hoping for some sign that rescue was on the way — a ship, a sail on the horizon. But nothing was there.

"I wonder if I'll ever be rescued?" she said aloud. Despite her best efforts, Georgie had not been able to stop talking to herself.

Climbing out of the tree, she shouldered her little makeshift pack and headed upstream, walking until it got too dark to see. For three more days she trudged on, sleeping at night in nests she made of dead leaves. The stream trickled along, much the same as it was near the beach. Occasionally trees and bushes grew so thick along its banks that Georgie was forced to walk in the stream itself. She saw rabbits, raccoons, deer, and of course, lots and lots of birds. But no people.

Finally Georgie turned back. She thought again about walking east along the coast to the borders of the United States. But there was still the problem of fresh water. Even if she filled the pitcher and carried it with her (and that would be mighty awkward), it would only hold so much. Not nearly enough for a long trip. There was no way of knowing when she would be able to refill it. It might be worth a chance, though. Georgie sighed and shook her head. She would have to put some more thought into this. She had lost track of the days, but she was certain it had been over a month and a half since the *Mary Maud* went down. Often it took much longer than that for word of a shipwreck to spread. It all depended on how long it took the survivors to reach civilization. Once again, she refused to consider the possibility that she alone had survived.

"No!" she said to a startled squirrel. "No. Jeff is alive. Mother and Father are alive. And Captain Davis. I'm not the only one. They *will* come and find me. They will."

As she approached the shore once again, Georgie was so deep in thought that she failed at first to notice the new sound that mingled with the birdsong and the swooshing of the surf. When it finally did catch her attention, she stood perfectly still with her head cocked to one side, listening intently.

Voices! She was certain she could hear people talking. Surely she was imagining it? No, there it was again. Somewhere nearby, people were talking to one another.

Rescue! She could not understand the words they said, but what did it matter? There were people on the beach. She was saved!

Georgie opened her mouth to hail her rescuers, but then she caught a glimpse of one of them through the trees. The cry died in her throat. The fellow did not look like any person she had ever seen. Careful not to make a sound, she gently put down her bundle and crept closer to the tree line to get a better look. There were several of them on the beach — and they were stark naked! Georgie blushed as she realized it. But she couldn't look away. They seemed to have some sort of designs painted on their skins. They had straight, reddish hair, and each carried a bow as tall as he was.

A memory tickled at the back of her mind. These must be the "heathen savages" Captain Davis had spoken of. Perhaps she *had* been blown all the way to Texas.

She wasn't saved. These men had not come to rescue her.

"Good heavens," she thought. "What do I do now?"

CHAPTER 8

· •) 〰 (• ·

Tunkutu was tense. Not afraid, certainly — that would be unworthy of a mighty warrior of the People. But he was wary. The pale, smelly foreigners had returned. All the signs said so — the neat shelter stacked with treasures; the stored food; the paths worn between the shelter, stream, and beach. Yet there was no one to be found. He could tell it was a small group — no more than three or four, surely. Perhaps only one. It was hard to know for certain. The signs were at least four or five days old, but the foreigners would certainly return to their shelter among the trees.

With his keen hunter's senses, he strained for any indication that the Pale Smelly Ones were nearby. Experience had taught the People that these Pale Ones were full of treachery. Many times they had been honored guests of the People, only to steal from their hosts at the first opportunity — canoes, dogs, food, even women. It seemed there was nothing these Pale Ones would not take if they desired it. The actual ownership of the items seemed not to matter to them at all.

They were strange, these foreigners — not at all like other tribes. They came in boats much bigger than the canoes used by the People. Yet those boats seemed unreliable — they often sank in the ocean and washed up on the shore. The People's canoes never wrecked. They might, perhaps, overturn in strong waves, but they never came apart like the boats made by these violent strangers. Of course, the People had enough sense not to go out in canoes during great storms. The Pale Ones seemed not to understand their danger. They sailed in the storms and often washed ashore with bits of their boats.

The People had learned to visit certain stretches of shoreline, like this one, after great storms. The wreckage of the Pale Ones' ships washed up in such places, and there were many useful and valuable things to be salvaged. Some items the People kept, others they traded with inland tribes.

The foreigners themselves were not so easy to deal with. They were unpredictable, often violent, and rarely to be trusted. Sometimes the People kept them as slaves. But usually they just killed the Pale Smelly Ones immediately. It was better — and far less trouble — that way. Occasionally the People made a meal of a captured foreigner, but Tunkutu didn't like the taste.

There was no doubt the foreigners would be returning to this place — they had stockpiled food and built a good shelter. They could return at any time, and they might have firesticks. So Tunkutu was especially alert. He knew he must kill the foreigners before they could kill any of the People here.

What was that? There was a rustling in the woods behind him. Tunkutu held very still, listening intently. He turned slowly, peering into the woods, his hands tightening on his bow. No man but he could draw this bow, and he would use it now to defend his warriors.

He heard the sound again. Something was moving stealthily across the forest floor. Tunkutu flexed his mighty bow, then fitted an arrow into place. With his left hand, he pulled back the bowstring and waited for his prey to emerge.

There!

Tunkutu stopped just before releasing his arrow and let loose a mighty laugh instead as he watched a squirrel dart out of the woods and scamper along the tree line. I am becoming as nervous as an old woman, he thought.

Still, something was making the hairs on the back of his neck stand up. He felt he was being watched. Tunkutu had been a hunter and warrior for too long to ignore that feeling. There was something in the woods — something bigger and more dangerous than a squirrel.

Turning again to face the sea, Tunkutu kept a tight grip on his bow and listened intently to the woods at his back. Something was making noise but trying not to. The warrior ran through the possibilities in his mind. Armadillo? Possibly, but they usually came out at dusk — not this time of day when the sky was bright. Coyote? Perhaps. Raccoon? No, they were creatures of the night.

This thing was clumsy, a creature moving in the woods that was unaccustomed to doing so. It *had* to be one of the Pale Smelly Ones. Nothing else made such a racket in the underbrush.

He casually took a few steps backward, toward the tree line. The small sounds behind him stopped, so he quit moving and listened carefully. He was sure he heard breathing and strained to pinpoint the sound. He was more certain than ever that a foreigner, or several, lurked in the woods behind him. His confidence grew. If they had firesticks, he said to himself, they would have used them by now. And if there were a great many of the Pale Smelly Ones, they probably would have attacked the small band of warriors. It was probably one or two frightened survivors from a shipwreck.

Tunkutu decided there was no reason to be cautious. He turned suddenly and rushed toward the spot along the edge of the forest where he thought he'd heard the breathing.

Something fled, crashing through the underbrush wildly as it tried to evade him. But it was no use. With only six giant steps Tunkutu intercepted the creature that had been watching the People from the woods.

A foreigner! But a small one. Why, it is only a child, Tunkutu thought. He had never seen children of the Pale Smelly Ones, but this was undoubtedly one of their young. Where were its parents? He tightened his grip on the squirming, squawking creature and began dragging it toward the beach, all the while scanning for signs of adults coming to its rescue.

By now the other warriors had noticed what was going on and gathered around Tunkutu and the foreign child.

"What are you waiting for, Tunkutu?" asked Dalawi. "Kill it."

"That one won't make much of a meal. It's too scrawny, not much meat on its bones," said Dalawi's brother, Rohana.

"Pah, who cares about eating it? It's one of the Pale Ones. Kill it now," said Murok.

Tunkutu said nothing as the other warriors argued about what to do with the child. Ordinarily he would have favored killing and eating an enemy. Better for the People to consume its power now than allow it to be used against them later. But there was something about this one that made him hesitate. It was, after all, only a child. It was not too late to teach it the proper ways. Besides, it would increase his prestige to have a slave. And his wife, Ulanga, was heavy with child — she would like having help with the chores.

His mind made up, Tunkutu spoke.

"It is I who captured the Pale One, and I who will decide its fate," he said.

The other warriors fell silent.

"The child will live in my ba-ak. It will serve me and Ulanga, and we will teach it the ways of the People."

"Foolishness!" snapped Murok. "It will grow up and betray you. These foreigners cannot be trusted. You know that, Tunkutu. We should kill and eat the creature now. Come, let us build a fire."

"No! The Pale One will serve in my household. Enough talk. I have decided," said Tunkutu. "We can always kill the child later if it shows signs of treachery."

CHAPTER 9

· • ⟩ ≋ ⟨ • ·

Georgie struggled in the grasp of the mighty warrior. He was, without a doubt, the biggest man she had ever seen. He was simply enormous — bigger even than Young Sven Freibold. And Young Sven was big — the biggest man in six counties, maybe in all of New York. The people back home joked that when he readied his fields for the spring planting, Young Sven dragged the plow while the mule walked along behind.

But this savage holding her was bigger than Sven. All the savages were huge, but the one holding her was the largest of the lot of them. They seemed to be arguing. Several gestured in her direction. She knew they must be trying to decide what to do with her.

I have to escape, she thought. But how?

She tried to twist away from the heathen holding her, but he only tightened his grip. The fingers of his left hand squeesed the tender flesh between her neck and shoulder until pain shot up her neck and down her back. With his right hand, the warrior twisted her arm firmly behind her back, holding her securely. For now, Georgie realized, she wasn't going anywhere this creature did not want her to go. She stopped struggling, but the warrior did not loosen his hold on her.

He said something to the other Indians that seemed to end their debate. Then he started pushing her along in front of him, down the beach toward her shelter. Several of the other warriors shot dark looks in Georgie's direction — looks that made her shiver — but they said nothing else.

"Let me go. You must let me go!" demanded Georgie, sounding much braver than she felt. She got no response.

She had heard terrible tales about the heathen savages who populated these shores. When the adults aboard the *Mary Maud* thought the children were sleeping or out of earshot, they talked in low voices about cannibals and brutal attacks that wiped out whole settlements. Captain Davis had said the natives were fierce and horrible, possessing no conscience and no mercy.

"Why, they'd just as soon kill you as look at you," he had said. "That's the way they are, completely uncivilized."

These warriors hadn't killed her yet, but she had been their captive for only a few minutes. Maybe they planned to have her for supper. The thought nearly paralyzed her with terror. She stumbled, and for a few steps, her captor dragged her across the sand. A harsh command and a sharp jerk on her arm made Georgie move her feet again. But she was still terribly frightened. A picture flashed through her mind of herself with an apple in her mouth, roasting over a fire like a pig on a spit.

Scanning the beach ahead of her, Georgie realized there was no fire. None of the savages seemed to be building one either. Perhaps they intend to eat me raw, she thought. That notion stilled her feet again, and with one despairing gasp she began to cry.

She could not stop herself. Tears coursed down her face, and her body shook with the force of her sobs. The savage stopped the forced march down the beach and let her go. Georgie dropped to her knees, still sobbing. Any minute, she knew, the warrior would strike her, slash her... kill her. Still crying, she waited for the fearsome blow. And waited... and waited. But it never came.

Instead, to Georgie's astonishment, the Indian sat on the sand in front of her and started crying too. Peering through her own tears, Georgie saw the savage's eyes were red and his cheeks were wet. He matched her, sob for sob, his voice occasionally soaring into a howling crescendo.

She couldn't believe it. What was going on? Was he mocking her? Was he sad to have to kill her? And what did the other Indians think of this? Georgie shot a look in their direction. They were standing in a group nearby, their faces impassive, waiting.

As she mulled it over, Georgie's sobs slowly subsided and her tears lessened. The warrior followed suit. He sat quietly, gazing at Georgie as she snuffled. Finally, he stood and gestured for her to do the same, saying a few words in a language she did not understand. Something seemed to have changed between them.

Georgie stood and walked with the warrior toward six sturdy canoes that had been pulled out of the water. The others followed, talking in low voices among themselves. As they neared the beached boats, Georgie saw that they had been piled with shipwreck debris. One bundle looked familiar — it was hers, the spare clothing she had scrounged her first week here! The Indians must have raided her shelter! All those things she had worked so hard to gather were gone — everything except the clothes she was wearing and the carefully wrapped knife. The Indians had not noticed it stuck in her waistband at the small of her back. The feel of it there comforted Georgie. Wherever she was going, a knife might come in handy.

Her captor dragged one of the canoes into the calm surf and pointed, first to her then to the front of the little craft. She nodded and scrambled into its bow. The warrior pushed it out past the breaker line, heaved himself into its stern, and then used a long pole to move them parallel with the coast.

Georgie gazed at the shore. A week ago she could think of nothing but getting away from that cursed stretch of beach. Now she eyed it longingly and felt a pang of what could only be homesickness. It was familiar. She had begun to feel safe there. Now she was leaving, the captive of these strange savages.

A gull screamed overhead, startling Georgie from her reverie.

"Easy for you to say," she said to the bird. "I wonder what will happen to me now?"

The canoes moved swiftly and soon left the exposed coastline for a shallow lagoon protected from the open sea by a long, narrow island. A breeze caressed Georgie's skin and the sun warmed her, from the short curls on her head to the bottoms of her dirty, bare feet. The heat, combined with the gentle motion of the canoes, coaxed her to close her eyes. Just for a minute, she thought. I'll just rest my.... But she never finished the thought, dropping instead into a deep sleep.

CHAPTER 10

· •) 〜 (• ·

A great jolt wrenched Georgie from her nap, and she was thrown onto her hands and knees in the front of the canoe. It took a few seconds for her to remember where she was. Then her captor slapped her on the shoulder and made a harsh sound she interpreted as, "Get out!"

She scrambled to her feet and stepped onto the damp sand, stopping abruptly as she came face to face with a short woman whose huge round belly indicated she'd be having a baby soon. The warrior stepped past Georgie and spoke to the woman, gesturing at Georgie as he talked. Not sure what to do, Georgie just stood there, staring.

After a brief conversation, the woman smiled and stepped toward Georgie as the warrior walked away without another glance at his captive. The pregnant Indian spewed a rapid string of words and then paused, as if waiting for an answer.

"I'm sorry, I don't understand," Georgie said.

The woman frowned and took a quick step toward Georgie while raising her hand. Instinctively, Georgie flinched. But the woman did not hit her. Instead, she pointed at Georgie, then at the canoe. Georgie, canoe, Georgie, canoe, Georgie, canoe.

Maybe the man had given her to this woman, and now the woman was going to take her somewhere else, Georgie thought.

"You want me to get back in the canoe?" she asked the Indian.

Georgie climbed back into the little boat and looked at the woman, who laughed, shook her head, and pointed to the mound of shipwreck debris piled in the little boat. When the Indian pointed once again in her direction, Georgie finally understood.

"Oh! You want me to unload the canoe. I can do that!"

When she grabbed a bundle and hopped out of the canoe, the woman smiled, nodded, and took another bundle for herself. Then she gestured for Georgie to follow as she headed up the beach toward a group of huts. When the Indian woman dropped her bundle on the ground outside one of them, Georgie did the same.

The woman pointed to herself and said a single word.

"Ulanga."

Then she waited.

"Ulanga," she said again, and pointed at Georgie.

Georgie didn't understand. She had done what the woman wanted her to do. What did "ulanga" mean? Indicating herself, Georgie said the word. Maybe the woman wanted her to ulanga something.

The woman shook her head and pointed to herself again.

"Oo-lan-ga," she said loudly and slowly, as if Georgie was deaf and very stupid.

"Oo-lan-ga," she said again, tapping her chest with an index finger.

And finally Georgie understood.

"Oh!" she said. "Ulanga. That's your name."

She pointed at the woman and said, "Ulanga?"

Ulanga nodded and pointed at Georgie.

"My name's Georgie," she replied, pointing to herself. "Georgie."

"Gor-gee," said Ulanga.

Close enough, thought Georgie, and nodded. "Georgie," she said.

Three times they made the trip back and forth to unload the canoe. Each time, more people joined them, though no one else touched the goods from the mighty warrior's boat. By the time they finished, there was a waist-high pile of stuff outside the hut and a crowd of women and children surrounding Georgie.

They stared at her, and she stared back at them. They weren't as dark-skinned as she had expected Indians to be, and like the men, their dark hair was rough and reddish. Many of them were tattooed like the sailors from the *Mary Maud*. From a distance it had looked as though the women were all grinning at her, but up close she could see they were not. In reality, their mouths were pierced all around with something — twigs, maybe, or bits of cane.

My, that must have hurt, she thought.

The children were all stark naked and very thin. Their ribs and collarbones were easy to see. The women wore skirts, some made of moss, others of animal hide, but all were bare from the waist up. As she watched, a child who looked to be six or seven years old went to its mother and began to suckle!

They truly are savages, thought Georgie. Where she came from the women and men were all decently covered and the children were weaned when they were toddlers.

One of the Indian women tentatively extended a finger and gently stroked Georgie's upper arm and then reached up to tug softly on one of her curls. Another woman darted close and smacked Georgie in the face.

Ulanga pushed between the other women and Georgie and spoke angrily to the one who'd hit her. An argument ensued, which Ulanga must have won because the others went away. Ulanga walked in the opposite direction and gestured for Georgie to follow her. Together they walked into the woods behind the camp. When Ulanga picked up a stick, Georgie did too.

Firewood, thought Georgie. We're gathering firewood. Why? It's not cold. We don't need a fire. It must be to cook something...Oh no, what if it's me?!

CHAPTER 11

· •) ≋ (• ·

Ulanga was worried. Why had Tunkutu not killed the strange foreign child? Why did he bring it home? It would be nice to have the help, of course — especially with a baby on the way. But they would also have to feed the Pale One, and there was barely enough food for the People as it was.

Gor-gee. It was an ugly thing, with odd hair the color of beach grass and eyes the color of a summer sky. Ulanga didn't even know if it was a boy or girl. Tunkutu had not said, and it was impossible to tell because of the clothes the child wore.

Glancing at it as they gathered firewood for that night's celebration, Ulanga had to admit it was a hard worker. Cheerful, too. But she feared its presence would bring doom on the People. What if the Spirits were displeased or its family came looking for it? The pale foreigners had always been bad luck for the People.

Badu was furious that a Pale Smelly One walked among them. Many seasons ago a foreigner had killed her father. Had Ulanga not interfered, she would have hit Gor-gee many more times or might even have strangled the child. But Badu had no right to do such a thing. Gor-gee belonged to Ulanga and Tunkutu. And Tunkutu had spoken. The child would live in their ba-ak and serve them.

With the child trailing behind her, Ulanga returned to the camp and started building a fire. When a nice blaze was crackling, she got the water pots from the ba-ak and showed Gor-gee where to fill them. This, she had decided, would be one of the foreigner's chores. She had always hated fetching water, and now she longer had to. Perhaps having this foreigner living with them wouldn't be so bad after all. Ulanga smiled.

With Gor-gee's help, she set out baskets of blackberries and the few fresh greens the women had been able to find. If the men were successful at fishing, they would have a fine party this night. The whole tribe would celebrate and honor the warriors who brought back so many fine things from the wreck of the foreign ship. Tunkutu, of course, would get the pick of the goods. It was he who found the shipwreck and he who discovered the foreign child. Pride swelled in Ulanga. Her husband was the best warrior and fisherman in the tribe. Everyone said so.

He will bring home many fish, she thought.

When Tunkutu arrived a few minutes later with six fish, Ulanga smiled. Yes, she thought, he is a fine man. I am very lucky.

The warrior settled onto a grass mat outside the ba-ak as Ulanga took the fish. She motioned for her new slave to come

near and began showing it how to prepare the fish for that
night's supper. But the child surprised her by taking the fish and
cleaning them as well as she could have done herself.

Perhaps these Pale Smelly Ones aren't completely uncivilized after all, Ulanga thought.

When she shared this observation with Tunkutu, he
nodded.

"Yes, there is more to these foreigners — or at least to this
one — than we suspected," he said. "This child knows the
Crying Ritual."

Ulanga was shocked. How could that be? The Crying Ritual
was one of the most sacred customs of the People.

"How do you know?" she asked her husband.

Tunkutu told her how the little slave had dropped cross-
legged on the sand and wept bitterly as he was taking it to his
canoe.

"Obviously, it was thanking me for sparing its life and taking it into my household," he said. "We exchanged no gifts, but
that would have been inappropriate between a slave and master
anyway. Have you discovered its name, Ulanga?"

"Yes," she said. "It is called Gor-gee," she said to her husband. "It's a bit stupid but works hard and is obedient. I thank
you for this gift, my husband."

Tunkutu was pleased but said nothing else. He only nodded.
That was the warrior's way. He did not need to brag. His actions
spoke for themselves. The little slave was there for all to see that
he was prosperous.

"Do you know if it's a girl or a boy?" Ulanga asked. She had
never seen one of these foreigners up close, but Tunkutu had.
He had killed many of them.

This question had not occurred to Tunkutu. He'd been thinking of it as the foreign child and the slave. He looked at Gor-gee. With its short hair and ragged trousers, the answer was obvious.

"It's a boy," Tunkutu said. "You can tell by the way it's dressed. Their women have long hair and wear long, foolish garments that tangle around the legs."

"Excuse me, Ulanga?"

Ulanga glanced up at the sound of her name. The little slave was holding out the cleaned fish for her approval. Ulanga took them and patted the child on the head.

"Do you think it knows we're talking about it?" she asked her husband.

"He, Ulanga. It's a boy," Tunkutu said. "And yes, I'm sure he knows. Look at the way he's watching us."

CHAPTER 12

Georgie could tell they were talking about her. She'd heard Ulanga mention her name. What were they saying? Now that she'd gotten used to their language, it didn't sound so harsh and horrible to her. These two, Ulanga and the warrior, were chatting pleasantly with an occasional glance in her direction. It reminded Georgie of how her parents used to talk as they sat by the fire after she and Jeff had gone to bed.

Georgie shook her head. How could she think that? How could she compare her wonderful parents to these ... these *savages*? The Indians were probably talking about the best way to torture her or prepare her for dinner. Once again, tears welled in her eyes as she imagined herself roasting over an open fire.

"Gor-gee!"

Georgie snapped out of her daydream. Ulanga was waving her over. The fire had been built up high and there were Indians of all ages standing there, at least thirty of them.

This is it, thought Georgie. I'll never see Jeff again.

But no one made a move toward her or raised a hand to her. No one even had a weapon, as far as she could see. Maybe they weren't going to kill her after all.

"Gor-gee!"

Ulanga said her name again, impatiently this time, and pointed into the hut. Georgie crawled inside and Ulanga shut the skin flap, leaving her alone in the darkness. Outside, the Indians began chanting. What did it mean?

It seemed like hours passed as she sat cross-legged in the darkness, listening to the commotion outside around the fire. At one point, a hand slid through the hut's flap, holding something. Georgie tensed and backed away. She fingered the knife in her waistband. But the hand retreated, leaving whatever it had held by the doorway. Curiosity overcame her fear, and Georgie crept toward the object. Her nose told her what it was before she got there. Food! As her mouth watered, Georgie realized she hadn't eaten since munching a bit of hardtack early that morning. Was it really the same day? So much had happened, Georgie could hardly believe it.

She snatched the bowl and dug into it with her fingers. It was too dark to see what she was eating, but her taste buds soon told her it was fish mixed with blackberries. Delicious! She'd seen the berries earlier, when she was working with Ulanga, but hadn't dared to eat one without permission. As she gobbled the contents of the bowl, Georgie realized it was the first real food she'd had since the shipwreck. By her calculations, it had been at least two months since she'd washed up on that beach.

She wondered if anyone had found her yellow dress yet. The Indians hadn't taken it — she'd seen it high in the tree as the canoes moved down the coast.

Too soon the bowl was empty, and Georgie set it aside. Outside, the singing went on and on. Finally, too tired to keep her eyes open any longer, Georgie curled up in a corner of the hut far from the door and allowed herself to drift to sleep.

She awoke with the feeling that someone was watching her, and when she opened her eyes, she found she was correct. A naked boy who looked to be about four years old sat near her head. When he saw she was awake, he giggled.

Georgie sat up. She was surrounded by sleeping Indians. Ulanga and the warrior who'd captured her were nearby, while another man and woman and two dogs snoozed on the other side of the hut.

Now was the time for her to escape! She crawled out of the hut, followed by the little boy. She tried to shoo him back inside, but he would not leave Georgie.

"Well, I don't suppose you'll be able to stop me. Come on then," she said to him.

She trotted down the beach toward the canoes but quickly realized she would not be able to handle one by herself. They were big and heavy. So she headed toward the tree line, giving the huts a wide berth. By now, two dogs had joined her and the little boy. The child took her hand and led her into the woods.

"Are you trying to help me escape?" she asked.

The child responded with a string of chatter in his language. He seemed eager and tugged at Georgie's hand to urge her along. Not knowing what else to do, Georgie followed the boy. Her spirits rose with every step until, all at once, the boy stopped and pointed with a big smile on his face.

Georgie's spirits fell. He had brought her to a berry bush. He wasn't helping her escape. He was showing her where to get breakfast.

"It's not that I don't appreciate it," she told him. "But I want to get away and find my own people."

The boy dropped her hand, plucked a few berries, and popped them in his mouth. Then he picked a few more and offered them to Georgie. Her stomach urged her to take them. Smiling, she did.

When Ulanga found them some time later, their hands and mouths were stained with berry juice and their bellies were full. Georgie realized she had missed her chance to escape.

CHAPTER 13

· •) ≋ (• ·

Many days passed before Georgie saw another chance to flee, but by then she had begun to wonder if she ought to. In truth, she wasn't even sure she was a prisoner. The People shared their food with her and treated her kindly for the most part. She was given chores, but she worked no harder than Ulanga or other members of the tribe.

No one guarded her, though four-year-old Godag had become her constant companion.

Georgie had to admit to herself that she liked the little boy. He was lively and charming and laughed a lot. When Tunkutu and Godag's father, Kronek, decided it was time to teach the child how to fish, he had insisted that Georgie go too.

So she found herself standing knee-deep in the ocean one day, holding a child-sized bow. Trying to copy the adults, she held very still and waited for fish to swim near. When one did, she loosed an arrow at it. Usually the fish got away and the arrow stuck, quivering, in the sand. But one glorious time the arrow struck home, and she snatched it from the water triumphantly with the fish still wiggling on it.

Godag whooped as if he had caught the fish himself and darted to the camp to tell of this great feat of fishing. He loved being the first to tell a bit of news. Tunkutu smiled and clapped her on the shoulder.

"Good, Gor-gee," he said.

Georgie smiled back. She had begun to learn the People's language, and this was a word she knew. Good. Tunkutu was pleased with her. That night they ate Georgie's fish along with those caught by Tunkutu, Kronek, and Godag. She was very proud and so eager for more practice that she was allowed to spend the whole of the next day fishing. This time she got two fish. But when she returned to the ba-ak to show Ulanga, Godag's mother would not let her enter.

"No," said Dooma. "You must go away."

A moan came from inside the ba-ak.

"Is Ulanga hurt?" Georgie asked.

"Ulanga's baby comes," Dooma said. "Go. This is no place for you. Take Godag with you and go."

Not knowing what else to do, Georgie sat by the fire with Godag, Tunkutu, and the other men, while the women of the tribe moved in and out of the ba-ak. After many hours, they heard the tiny crying of a newborn. Tunkutu smiled and Kronek slapped him on the back.

"Rejoice in the cry of a healthy child, my brother! You are a father. I congratulate you!"

After he had accepted congratulations from all the men, Tunkutu went to the ba-ak to see Ulanga and his first child. He returned a few minutes later.

"The baby is a girl. She shall be a credit to the People," he said. But Georgie could tell he was disappointed. Tunkutu had wanted a son.

Several weeks later, Ulanga summoned Georgie.

"Congratulations," she said. "You are to be adopted."

"What?" asked Georgie, not sure she understood the word. "What do you mean 'adopted'?"

"Tunkutu wants a son and I have failed to give him one. In you he sees the son he wishes to have. So at the next full moon there will be a great celebration, and you will become a member of our family. Ever after, I will be your mother and Tunkutu will be your father. You will be a warrior of the People."

Georgie left the ba-ak trying to sort out what she'd heard. She hadn't understood every word, but she thought Ulanga had told her she was being adopted as a member of the tribe.

Godag confirmed her suspicions when he raced up to her, whooping and hollering. "We are to be cousins, Gor-gee! You will become one of the People! We will have great adventures together!"

Not everyone was as happy about it as Godag. Some muttered darkly about foreigners bringing doom on the tribe or weakening its bloodlines. But Tunkutu would hear no opposition. He pointed to the unusually good hunting the tribe had enjoyed since Georgie joined them. He had made up his mind, and the shaman had agreed. No one asked Georgie what she thought.

On the day of the adoption, Ulanga told her to go wash herself and return to the ba-ak. When she did, Georgie found

Ulanga, Tunkutu, and the shaman waiting for her with paints and ornaments to prepare her for the ceremony. She was mortified when Ulanga told her to take off her clothes. There were men present!

She started to argue, but Ulanga shook her head and said in a firm voice, "You are to become one of the People. You will dress as one of the People. If you do not undress, I will cut the clothes from your body."

Georgie certainly didn't want that. She wanted to keep them for when she was rescued. Reluctantly, she turned her back and took off her clothes. When she turned around, the onlookers gasped. Georgie blushed. She felt she'd die of embarrassment.

Ulanga picked up a pabigo, one of the flimsy deerhide skirts worn by the women of the tribe, and gave it to Georgie.

"Put this on," she said kindly.

Tunkutu and the shaman were talking in furious whispers.

"Ulanga, what's happening?" Georgie asked, as she slipped into the garment.

"Oh, Gor-gee, we thought you were a boy. Tunkutu wanted a son. That is why he was adopting you. Tunkutu never would have let you touch a bow if he'd known you were a girl. He is afraid this will make him lose face with the tribe."

And finally Georgie understood the word that had so mystified her. *A son.* Ulanga's baby was a girl, but Tunkutu had wanted a son. All this time, they'd thought she was a boy. That's why he'd taught her to fish. That's why she hadn't been helping the women with their work.

Tunkutu looked angry — angry enough to hurt her. But Ulanga put a comforting arm on her shoulder.

"No harm will come to you, Gor-gee," she said. "Fear not. You are safe with me."

Tunkutu glanced again in their direction, and his expression seemed to soften. He spoke again with the shaman, who nodded.

"Ulanga," whispered Georgie, pointing at her shirt and trousers. "Can I put my old clothes back on, now that I'm not being adopted?" She felt terribly exposed.

"Oh, but you will still be adopted," said Ulanga, who had been eavesdropping on her husband and the shaman. "Hush now. Let Tunkutu tell you."

Georgie turned to face the warrior and the shaman, who had come up behind her.

"Gor-gee, you shall be the daughter of Tunkutu. You will be a woman of the People and mother of great warriors," said the shaman. "Be mindful of the honor bestowed on you."

With that, he took a puff from an ornate pipe he held in his left hand. He bent close to Georgie and blew the smoke in her left ear. He repeated the process with the other ear, and then he had her open her mouth and suck in the smoke he exhaled.

She coughed and her eyes watered. As she blinked away tears, Georgie could have sworn the shaman was smiling a little. But when she looked again he was stern and grim once more. The shaman lifted a staff in his right hand and touched her gently on the top of her head with it. Then he turned and crawled out of the ba-ak with Tunkutu. Ulanga quickly took his place in front of Georgie, dipped her finger in a pot of black paint, and starting in the middle of her forehead, drew a straight line from her hairline to her chin. Then she picked up a necklace made of shells and placed it around Georgie's neck.

Outside, the shaman was speaking.

"...and so, through the powers of the spirits, the foreign child Gor-gee becomes a child of the People. Emerge, daughter of Tunkutu!"

Ulanga pushed Georgie toward the ba-ak's flap. Georgie crawled through, blinking into the firelight, and stood beside Tunkutu. Ulanga followed.

"Behold, my daughter," said Tunkutu.

Georgie cringed under their stares. She felt so naked. Probably because I *am* naked, she thought.

The members of the tribe gazed at her uncertainly. Georgie thought she understood their confusion. They'd been expecting a son, a warrior to increase their strength against enemies.

After a few uncomfortable moments, Gordag stepped forward, handed her a shiny black feather, and said, "Welcome, sister." One by one, the other members of the tribe followed suit and welcomed her with gifts. A few made quick trips to their own ba-aks before approaching. Georgie guessed they were exchanging presents intended for a boy with items considered more appropriate for a girl. By the time the ceremony was over, two baskets, a clay pot, several beads and bone sewing needles, a flint, several hides, and an odd, sharpened stick had joined Gordag's feather in a pile at her feet.

Ulanga leaned over and whispered in her ear: "You must thank them. Offer to share your goods and vow to be true to the People."

Georgie did exactly as her foster mother instructed.

By the time she curled up on her skins in the ba-ak that night, Georgie was a full-fledged member of the People. She hadn't wanted to be adopted, but what choice did she have?

CHAPTER 14

· •) ⋙ (• ·

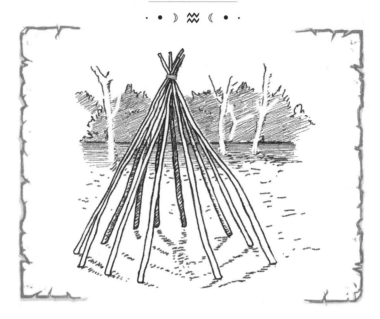

The tribe broke camp and moved a few days after the adoption ceremony. Ulanga showed Georgie how to dismantle the ba-ak and pack all the family's goods into Tunkutu's canoe. When everyone was ready to go, Ulanga climbed into the sturdy boat with baby Borami. Georgie and Tunkutu pushed the canoe into the calm bay, scrambled aboard, and they were off — a dozen canoes carrying the People west. A half day's journey brought them to another small island.

Ulanga and Dooma left Georgie to set up the ba-ak while they went looking for berries and other edible plants. It was a struggle — the other ba-aks were in place long before Georgie finished. First she laid out twelve slender willow poles, each three times as long as a man is tall. Each pole had a sharpened end, which she forced into the soft ground one at a time in a circular pattern. She laced the other ends of the poles together overhead and tied them with hide thongs and sinews. Finally she threw woven mats and skins over the framework she'd built. Standing back, she gazed with satisfaction at her handiwork. It was a little lopsided, but it was sturdy. And she had done it all by herself.

Over the next several months, she became quite adept at handling the ba-ak as the People moved from place to place. They usually camped on the shores of lagoons or on the sandy little barrier islands. On days when they weren't moving, Georgie fetched water and gathered plants. She learned that the sharpened stick she'd been given the night of her adoption was for digging roots. Dooma and Ulanga taught her to make baskets and pottery bowls and jars that they used for storing food and water and for cooking. They also showed her how to waterproof the containers with the lumps of gooey black stuff they gathered on the beach.

Georgie cooked and kept the camp tidy and cared for Gordag and Borami — all the traditional chores reserved for the women of the People. No matter how hard she begged Tunkutu, he would never take her hunting or fishing again. He had been teased a great deal by the other warriors for teaching a woman to fish and had no desire to go through that again. Occasionally, when no one else was around, Gordag would let her practice with his small bow. The women were allowed to set snares for small animals like rabbits, but Georgie hated to see the little creatures struggling in the nooses she set.

From time to time, she thought about running away from the People. But she had no idea where to go. She'd seen no signs of white settlements. Kronek had told her the closest one was many days' journey away, on Snake Island in a great harbor.

When she pressed him for more information, he clammed up and refused to say more. Worse than that, he reported the conversation to his brother, Tunkutu.

"Gor-gee, why do you seek the village of the Pale Smelly Ones?" he asked her.

In all her time with the People, only Gordag had ever asked about her life before Tunkutu found her. So she told her adoptive parents about her other family and how she longed to find them.

They listened, but Tunkutu started shaking his head before she finished speaking.

"They are dead, Gor-gee. The ocean took them. You must accept that," he said. "You are a member of the People now. We are your family. We will not speak of this again."

As summer arrived in force, the People struck camp once again. But this time they headed inland and settled in a thicket near a great marsh. Georgie hated it and did not understand why they'd left the coast with its cooling breezes for this hot, swampy place. Insects plagued her, even when she relented and allowed Ulanga to apply a foul-smelling grease made from shark liver to her skin.

She was sitting outside the ba-ak one day, slapping at the pesky bugs and weaving a mat, when she heard a commotion on the far side of the camp. It was heading in her direction. Georgie got to her feet just as Dooma came into view carrying Gordag. Something had happened to him!

Dooma handed her son to Georgie and left in search of the shaman. Georgie saw at once that her young friend was very ill indeed. His skin was hot and clammy, and his eyes had rolled back in his head. He did not respond when she shook him gently or called his name. She maneuvered the child into the ba-ak and made him as comfortable as she could. Remembering what Jeff had done for her when she was sick with scarlet fever, she dipped a rabbit skin in a jar of water and bathed Gordag's face with it until help arrived.

The shaman carefully examined the boy and told Georgie to build a fire in the ba-ak's hearth. While she got a blaze going, he laid his hands on Gordag's head and chest and breathed on the boy from his forehead to his toes. When the fire had burned down to coals, the shaman took half a dozen palm-sized stones from a bag he'd brought with him and put them in the embers. After several minutes, he used his staff to rake them out. When they were cool enough for him to pick up with his bare hands, he placed one on Gordag's head and arranged the others in a curlicue pattern on his chest. He told Georgie to build the fire back up, tossed a handful of leaves on it, and shooed her and Dooma out as acrid smoke filled the ba-ak.

The shaman stayed with Gordag in the ba-ak while the family waited outside. They heard him chant and smelled the herbs he burned. But at the end of the third day, the shaman emerged and shook his head. Gordag was dead.

Dooma's howl pierced the evening, followed quickly by Kronek's. Tunkutu and Ulanga joined them and, after a moment's hesitation, so did Georgie. It didn't take much effort. She was heartbroken. Charming, lighthearted little Gordag — her first and best friend among the People — was gone forever.

They buried him in a shallow grave. Every day the family gathered at dawn, midday, and sunset to weep for Gordag. The People were very serious about their crying. It was a way of honoring one another, and much ceremony accompanied it. Ulanga had explained it all to Georgie. They would continue the thrice-daily crying sessions for one year. The mourning period would not be over until they had purified themselves with smoke. It was hard for Georgie to weep on demand — she felt cried out after the second day. When she couldn't summon tears, she would hide her face in her hands and make loud sobbing sounds. If anyone noticed her deception, they never mentioned it. She thought it a strange tradition, but not as odd as the prohibition against food gathering. Ulanga had explained that to her, too: When a man or boy child died, the family could not hunt or gather food for three months. It was up to the others in the camp to feed the family.

"But what if they don't have enough to share?" asked Georgie.

"Then we don't eat."

By the time the People broke camp to head back for the coastline several weeks later, Georgie had gone hungry only twice. The others in the camp had been generous with Gordag's family.

She was glad for the activity necessitated by the move. She had never realized how much time was spent just finding food. There was precious little for her to do with that duty gone.

The leaves were turning scarlet and yellow by the time they could gather and hunt again. Georgie, Ulanga, and Dooma dug the roots of water plants, caught fish in cane weirs, and set snares for rabbits, birds, and other small animals. The warriors fanned out looking for bigger game. Georgie and Ulanga were proud when Tunkutu returned to camp one day with a great fat doe slung across his shoulders. The deer would feed the whole camp for a week.

The People planned a great mitote, a celebration, in his honor. Georgie was excited. First the women built a special hut just for the occasion. Then the men made a special tea from yaupon leaves. Ulanga warned Georgie not to go near the men while the tea-making was going on, but her curiosity got the better of her. She crept near enough to see a yellow, frothy liquid bubbling away in a pot. Georgie was backing away quietly when a large hand jerked her to her feet.

"Do not drink the tea!" cried Dalawi as he held the struggling girl. "A woman has seen it cooking!"

The warriors gathered around Dalawi and an embarrassed Georgie.

"Gor-gee! You have brought shame on me!" thundered Tunkutu. "A warrior of the People could sicken and die if a woman passes while the tea is uncovered."

Dalawi handed Georgie over to Tunkutu and stomped off toward the ceremonial hut. As Tunkutu dragged her into the woods, Georgie saw Dalawi dump out the tea. Tunkutu stooped and picked up a long, thin stick.

"I will teach you to dishonor the ways of the People," he said, releasing Georgie and hitting her with the stick. She scrambled away from him, but he followed her, swinging the stick. Tunkutu landed more than fifty blows before he stopped the beating. Then he dropped the stick in disgust and walked away without another word for his adopted daughter.

Georgie ached all over, and her nose was gushing blood. She curled into a tight ball with her hands to her face and cried. Ulanga found her several hours later and helped her get back to the ba-ak. As she washed the blood from Georgie's face, they heard one of the warriors call out, "Who wishes to drink?"

Ulanga froze.

"Gor-gee, do not move," she whispered. "Do not speak, either, unless you want another beating."

Georgie didn't. She stayed perfectly still until Ulanga told her the men had finished drinking. That night the women built a great fire and served supper to the men. Then they stood at a distance with their hair over their faces as the men danced and made music with whistles and tortoiseshell tambourines.

Georgie stood with the rest of the women, miserable and disappointed. She had been so excited about this festival, but the women weren't allowed to participate at all! Worse yet, she had shamed Tunkutu. She couldn't wait for it to be over. For three days the women were on constant alert for the cry of "Who wishes to drink?" She spent most of that time devising ways to escape from the People. By the time the mitote ended, Georgie's bruises had turned purple and green and she was resolved on leaving.

But something always seemed to come up. Borami was frequently in her care, and she could hardly run off with a baby. Or they spent an entire day in the canoe moving to a new campsite. There was always something that kept her from going. On particularly fine days, she often forgot she intended to escape until the opportunity had passed.

Before she knew it, winter was upon the People. They huddled under mounds of skins at night, but during the day they donned no more clothing than they wore in summer — despite the frigid temperatures. Georgie couldn't understand why the tribe would live on the exposed shoreline when it was so cold and then move inland away from the cool coastal breezes in the summer. But when she asked, Ulanga only shrugged and said that was how it had always been for the People.

How Georgie longed for her warm woolen cloak! But with the exception of the knife and the clothes she was wearing the day Tunkutu caught her, her treasures from the shipwreck had long since been parceled out among the People. She begged Ulanga to let her don the old shirt and trousers and nearly wept with gratitude when she agreed. The clothes were a bit small for her but felt wonderful all the same.

She was careful to always take them off before wading out to the oyster beds with Ulanga, a trip they made nearly every day. The People existed almost totally on oysters during the winter. There was little else to eat, and many of the People sickened.

One sad day, Dalawi's daughter died of a fever. But the People did not have enough food to share with the grieving family. Dalawi, his wife, and their young son soon followed her to the grave.

By the time the berries returned to the woods, Georgie was very thin. Along with the rest of the People, she gorged herself on spring's bounty. She hoped never to eat another oyster as long as she lived.

As was their custom, the People continued to move from campsite to campsite, and one day they arrived on a long, sandy island that separated a shallow bay from the open ocean. Georgie thought there was something familiar about it, but so many of these inlets looked alike to her that she shrugged off the feeling.

Two days later, after an intense thunderbumper, she and ten others accompanied Tunkutu to scavenge a stretch of shoreline for shipwreck debris. It wasn't until she saw the tattered, faded remnants of her dress high in a tree that she knew where she was — back on the beach where the People had found her.

As she gazed at the yellow rag, Georgie realized more than a year had passed since the *Mary Maud* had sunk. A year. A whole year. That meant she was eleven now. Jeff would be twelve — if he was still alive.

"He is! I know he is!" she said to a startled squirrel.

Shading her eyes with one hand, Georgie gazed out to sea hoping to see a ship or a sail. But nothing was there, except the endless sea and great expanse of blue sky.

CHAPTER 15

· • ⟩ ≈ ⟨ • ·

As the days grew warmer, Georgie's determination to leave the People and try to find her family grew, too.

She knew better than to broach the subject with Tunkutu. He would only say that her other family was dead. She knew that might be true, but even if it was, she wanted to get back to civilization.

"It should be my choice," she told a blackbird.

To the habit of talking to herself, Georgie had added the habit of talking to the birds and beasts around her. Only now she spoke in the language of the People, not in English.

The bird squawked back at her in the language of its kin. She chose to believe he was saying, "Of course it should. You are absolutely right!" That was one of the advantages of talking with animals, she thought; they always agreed with you. Georgie grinned at the thought.

"You seem happy today, my daughter," said Ulanga.

"It is a beautiful day. We have plenty to eat and everyone is well. I am happy," Georgie replied.

She felt a little guilty. Ulanga had always been good to her and here she was, plotting to run away. Not only that, she'd been stealing things from the ba-ak to help her on the journey: a small clay pot, thongs, a few skins and sewing needles, a digging stick, Gordag's small bow, and some arrows. She kept it all in a bag she'd made from a bit of deerskin and hidden outside the camp. Each time they moved she retrieved the bag and packed it with her belongings, then she found a hiding place near the new camp. Some of the items belonged to her, and she told herself that she had the right to take the others since she worked so hard for Tunkutu and Ulanga. But Georgie never quite managed to convince herself. It still felt like stealing.

She had decided she must leave before the People moved inland for the summer. By her calculations, that gave her at least two months to slip away. There would be no problem finding food and water now — after living with the People for so long, she knew what to look for. And she had gathered everything she thought she would need from the ba-ak — she resolutely pushed the word "stolen" from her mind. The only thing left to do, it seemed, was to go.

She would choose her time carefully, leaving the camp right after the morning cry for Gordag. They would be angry when she did not show up for the midday cry, but they would not think to look for her until the evening. Even then, she knew, they would be worried some accident had befallen her. It would take at least a day or two before they suspected she had deliberately fled, and by then she would have a good head start. She'd go east, toward the borders of the United States, since they were likely to think she'd gone the other way in search of the settlement Kronek had told her about.

But before she could execute her plan, everything changed.

Murok rushed into camp one morning calling out, "Beware! Beware! The enemy approaches!" He had been gone several days on a hunt.

The warriors crowded around him, all asking questions at once. Tunkutu raised his hand for silence. "Tell us, Murok. What have you seen?"

"Foreigners! A ship of the Pale Ones approaches!"

All eyes turned to the ocean, but there was nothing out of the ordinary there.

"Where, Murok? There is nothing there. Perhaps you saw something else," said the shaman.

"I am a warrior of the People," Murok replied. "I do not make such mistakes."

At that moment, a child cried out. All eyes turned again to the ocean, and this time all could see that Murok was right. A great wooden vessel with white sails appeared on the horizon. The boat was headed in their direction.

Georgie's heart leapt! Rescue!

"Come, Gor-gee," Ulanga said, laying a hand on her shoulder. "Hurry. We must hide."

It didn't take long because they weren't going far, just a few hundred yards to a clearing in the woods where the foreigners couldn't see them.

We'll be safe from them here, Georgie thought, and then wanted to slap herself. What had gotten into her? I *am* one of them, she thought, not one of the People. Good grief!

While the women and children moved the camp, the men prepared for war. They hid the canoes and gathered their weapons — clubs and lances and bows. They painted their faces black and red. In the dying sunlight, the warriors looked ferocious. Georgie shuddered and jumped when Ulanga laid a hand on her shoulder.

"Do not worry, child. If the foreigners do not bother us, nothing will happen," she said.

By now the ship had sailed close to shore and anchored far down the beach from where the People had been camped. Murok, who had been sent to spy on the Pale Ones, returned with disturbing news.

"They are coming ashore in small wooden boats," he said. "They have many firesticks."

"The People know from experience what that means," said Tunkutu. "The Pale Ones are here to steal from us and to kill. We must attack them first, take them by surprise."

There was a general murmur of agreement among the men. It took them only a few minutes to choose a course of action: make war on the Pale Ones. They chose Tunkutu to lead the attack.

Georgie watched with a sinking heart as the warriors disappeared into the woods with the shaman. What if Father was on that boat? I have to do something, she thought. But what? Obviously, she had to warn the men from the ship.

· · ■ ☠ ■ · ·

CHAPTER 16

"**G**or-gee!"

Georgie whirled to see Ulanga standing behind her.

"Come, child."

Oh no, thought Georgie. What now? I have to get away from here. I have to warn them.

"Ulanga, where are we going?" she asked.

"Quickly! And be quiet. If you want to join the foreigners, do as I say."

Georgie could hardly believe what she heard.

"Ulanga?"

"Ssssshhh."

Georgie trotted down the beach after her. They were careful to stay just inside the tree line, where no one could see them. Georgie's heart pounded with every step. When they were several hundred yards from where the Pale Ones had landed, the Indian woman pulled her into the trees.

"From here you must go alone," Ulanga said. "But you must hurry."

"Ulanga, what are you doing? Tunkutu and the others will be here any second. They'll see you."

"No, child. The shaman must bless them first. Then they will boast, telling one another how courageous they are. Only then will they attack." She spat on the ground. "The fools. These foreigners have done nothing to them, yet they will risk the firesticks to attack. It is a stupid, senseless way to die. We have a little time, but not much. Go now. You will save Tunkutu if you do."

Tears welled in Georgie's eyes. For months, she'd thought of nothing but escape. Presented now with that very opportunity, she was reluctant to go. Ulanga had been so good to her. If she left now, Georgie knew she would never see her Indian family again.

"Gor-gee, you have been a good daughter, a joy to me. But you must go. It is the best thing. You must get the foreigners away from here for the sake of us all," said Ulanga. "I will tell the others you were stolen by the Pale Ones so they will not wonder why I am here. But this will stir their anger. Go now. The warriors are coming!"

Georgie threw her arms around Ulanga and hugged the startled woman. Then she leaped to her feet and darted onto the beach without looking back. As she ran, she counted two boats and six men. They hadn't seen her yet. It occurred to her to be glad that she'd never gone back to wearing the pabigo. Her shirt and trousers were too small, but at least they covered her decently.

"Hello!" she yelled. "Help! You're in danger! Hurry!" As the words tumbled out, she suddenly realized she'd spoken in the language of the People. She tried again, this time calling out in English. The words sounded odd to her after so long.

"Danger!" she yelled as she neared the first man. "You're in danger!"

He turned in a panic, slashing with a great knife in his right hand, missing Georgie's arm by the width of a cat's whisker. She stopped abruptly, staring wide-eyed at him. He was a mountain of a man — as big as Tunkutu — with sleek black hair and a beard shot through with gray.

"By the saints, where did you come from?" he asked, putting the knife back in its sheath.

"No time," gasped Georgie. "The warriors are coming. You have to get off the beach!"

"What?" asked the sailor.

Georgie shook her head and began pushing the fellow toward the boats. Behind her she heard Ulanga's voice raise the alarm.

"Help! The Pale Ones have stolen Gor-gee!"

Georgie knew the war party must be near. Seconds were critical now.

"We're in danger! We have to go! Now!" she said.

The man scooped Georgie into his arms and ran toward the boats. He let out a long whistle and yelled, "Come on, lads! Make haste! Trouble's on the way!"

The men converged on the boats — the six men Georgie had seen and three more that she hadn't. They stared at Georgie, but her companion's demeanor convinced them to ask questions later. He dumped her unceremoniously into the nearest boat and began dragging it into the surf. Four men helped him while the other five dealt with the second craft. Once the boats were afloat, they climbed in. Two men in each grabbed the oars and began hauling on them.

"What's this all about, Bron?" a skinny fellow asked the big man.

"Well now, that's the question to be sure," the big fellow answered. "The lad there came runnin' at me from out o' nowhere, screamin' at the top o' his lungs that we were in danger. All things considered, I was in no mood to argue."

Georgie opened her mouth to explain. But before she was able to say a single word, a terrible screech split the air and the warriors of the People poured onto the beach from the forest.

"Kronks!" yelled Bron. "Pull, lads! Pull! Your lives depend on it!"

The men at the oars redoubled their efforts. Bron barked orders.

"Johnny, get ready with your rifle," he said. "Don't fire unless the savages are right up on us. Make it count. You won't have time to reload."

The man called Johnny nodded and put a long gun to his shoulder. Looking past him, Georgie could see the warriors running into the surf. They howled in frustration as their prey escaped. One of them — Georgie thought it was Murok — lifted his bow and loosed an arrow. His aim was deadly. A man in the second boat clutched his midsection as the arrow passed completely through his body and pinned him to the side of the boat.

Encouraged, the warriors launched more arrows, but darkness was falling and the boats were far out from the shore. The arrows plopped uselessly into the waters of the lagoon. Loathe to give up the chase, several of the warriors started swimming after the boats, but they turned back when Johnny popped a shot in their direction.

Bron turned to Georgie. "Well, laddie, from the looks of you, you've got quite a story to tell."

Georgie nodded, but she didn't know where to start. She realized that they all thought she was a boy. Remembering what had happened with the People, she figured that was just as well — at least until she found out more about these folks. Boys sure got treated better than girls out here on the frontier, she thought.

At that moment, it hit her. Rescued! She'd been *rescued*! It was obvious these men hadn't come looking for her, but they might be able to help her find her family.

"I don't suppose my father is with you?" she asked hopefully.

"Well I dunno. Who's your Da'? Or do you want me to guess?" asked Bron. He spoke with a rolling Irish brogue, and his warm brown eyes crinkled at the edges when he smiled as he did at that moment. Georgie liked him. She smiled back.

"Johnson. James Johnson is his name. We were on the *Mary Maud* last year when it sank," she said.

"The *Mary Maud*, eh? Any of you fellows heard of the *Mary Maud*?" asked Bron. The sailors around her shook their heads. Georgie's spirits sank, and it must have showed on her face because Bron quickly said, "Never you mind. I'll wager the captain has heard o' her."

"Now then," he said. "We know the names o' your ship and your sire. Is it permitted to know the name of he who saved our sorry hides today?"

"Georgie. I'm Georgie Johnson," she said. It felt strange to be talking in English.

"Well it's pleased I am to make your acquaintance, Master George," he said. "I'm Bronson, Blackie Bronson if you please, mate on the *Jupiter*. And speakin' o' that fine ship, here we are now. Ahoy the *Jupiter*!"

They were taken aboard in short order, and Bronson went in search of the captain. The poor fellow who'd taken the arrow had died quickly, and his body was laid out on the deck. The other members of the landing party filled in the crew about that evening's activities on the beach. Georgie found she was the object of many curious glances, though no one spoke to her. But she was not alone for long.

In a few minutes Bronson returned, followed by a handsome, middle-aged man dressed entirely in black.

"My dear boy, do allow me to introduce myself," the gentleman said. "Jean Lafitte, at your service. Welcome aboard the *Jupiter*."

· ● ■ ☠ ■ ● · ·

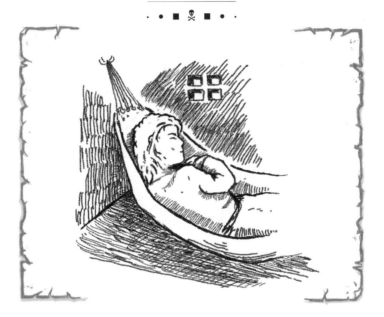

CHAPTER 17

Georgie didn't believe her ears — or eyes. Even back in New York they'd heard tales of the fearsome Lafitte — a dashing pirate who slept on a bed of gold coins looted from Spanish ships. He was the terror of the Gulf of Mexico and the scourge of Spain. How could this pleasant man with gray-speckled hair be him?

"Jean Lafitte, the pirate?" Georgie blurted.

"Pirate? Certainly not!" said the man indignantly. "I am a patriot and a businessman. A *privateer*, perhaps, but not a pirate. Now then, would you care to tell me who you are and where you came from?"

"My name is Georgie Johnson, and I was with my family on the *Mary Maud* when a storm wrecked us."

"The *Mary Maud*. That's a passenger ship?"

Georgie nodded.

"It doesn't sound familiar," he said. And Georgie's spirits sank.

"When did this happen?" Lafitte inquired.

"Last year. February, I think," she replied.

"And what happened to the rest of the survivors? Did the Kronks get them? Or are they someplace in hiding?"

"Kronks?" said Georgie. "What's a Kronk?"

"Kronks! Karankawas...the Indians who attacked you today," Lafitte said impatiently.

"Oh, you mean the People," said Georgie, using the word the Indians used for themselves.

"Are the other survivors with them?" asked Lafitte.

"No," said Georgie. "There were no others. It was just me."

A murmur swept through the crowd of sailors at this bit of news.

"Do you mean to say you survived this twelvemonth and more on your own — and managed to avoid the Kronks too?" asked Bronson.

"Oh no. It wasn't like that at all," said Georgie. Then she related the tale of the shipwreck and how she'd been separated from the others and adopted by the People.

"Astonishing," Lafitte said when she finished. "I've never heard of this *Mary Maud*, but many ships founder along this coast. When we get back to Campeachy, I'll make some inquiries."

"What's Campeachy?" Georgie asked.

"Ah, it's an oasis it is, a veritable paradise on the Gulf," said Bronson.

"It's my colony in Texas, on Snake Island," said Lafitte. "Now then, let's get you a meal and some decent clothes. I'm sure we have something around here that will fit you."

Almost before she knew it, Georgie was full and warm and as clean as she could get with only a pitcher of water and a basin to wash in. Bronson hung a hammock for her in the captain's quarters, and she was soon stretched out and dozing off to the *Jupiter*'s rocking.

Georgie must have been more tired than she realized. When she awoke, an entire day had passed and the sun was setting again. I must be making up for lost sleep, she thought.

"Ah, awake at last," said Lafitte as he ducked into the room. "Get up, young George. I want you to meet someone."

She rolled out of the hammock and landed with a thud on the wooden planks.

"Here," said Lafitte as he handed over a small, round mirror. "Meet my new cabin boy."

Georgie didn't understand what he was saying at first, and then it dawned on her.

"Me?" she asked.

"Yes," said Lafitte. "Welcome aboard."

CHAPTER 18

· • ■ ☠ ■ • ·

From cannibals to pirates — what next?! Georgie was afraid to even think about it.

Being a cabin boy wasn't so bad. She had to serve Lafitte's meals, keep his quarters clean, and take care of his clothes. She had never met a man so fussy about how he looked. Come to think of it, she hadn't known many women who were as persnickety as he was.

The hardest part of this new life was hiding her own gender. There wasn't a lot of privacy aboard a ship, and she was finding it increasingly difficult to keep the crew from finding out she was a girl.

She never left Lafitte's quarters if she could avoid it. Not all the sailors were as nice as Bronson. Some of them made her nervous. Others just flat scared her. But Bronson quickly became her friend. She simply adored the Irishman. He always had a joke or a song on his lips. He called her Cannibal Lad and Georgie Porgie and thanked her at least once a day for "saving my no-good skin."

"I know 'tis not much to look at," he'd say. "But 'tis the only one I've got, and I'm rather fond of it."

"I suppose he reminds me of Jeff," she said aloud. She was still in the habit of talking to herself. No animals to chat with here, unless you counted the rats — great, whopping big ones — that infested the ship.

Three days after she joined the crew, Bronson popped into Lafitte's cabin to ask if she knew how to use a gun.

"Yes," she said. "Father taught Jeff and me how to shoot before we left New York."

"Good," said Bron. He shoved a rifle into her hands along with some extra powder and ammunition. "We're going to do some business, George. Stay here. I'm going to lock you in. But I want you to be able to protect yourself if you have to."

"Bronson, wait!" she called.

But he was gone. Georgie shuddered to think what kind of "business" they were about to conduct. Lafitte's cabin had a window so she scrambled to it. But there was nothing to see but the ocean and the sky.

Hearing, though, that was different. First she heard the ship's cannons boom. They were firing on another ship! The realization took her breath away. Then came another, similar sound — the other ship must be firing back. Soon she heard shouting and felt a great jolt. Then there was silence.

She checked the rifle to make sure it was ready to fire and aimed it at the door. When she heard footsteps, she grasped the gun firmly and sighted down the barrel. The sound stopped just outside the cabin. Whatever it was, Georgie was ready.

"Wait, Captain! Wait!" Bronson yelled. "Georgie's got a gun, and if I know him it's trained on that doorway!"

Georgie laughed as she lowered the firearm.

"Come on in," she said. "You're safe from me."

Lafitte entered, followed by Bronson.

"It was good thinking to arm the boy," Lafitte said to his mate. "It was even better to warn me you had!"

They all laughed. Then Georgie's curiosity got the better of her, and she asked what had just happened.

"Oh, we liberated some gold and other goodies from a Spanish ship," said Bronson.

She didn't ask what had happened to the Spanish crew. She really didn't want to know.

As if reading her mind, Bronson said, "You probably ought to stay down here awhile." She only nodded, grateful to him for warning her.

In very short order they had had two more "liberating" — and profitable — encounters with Spanish vessels, so the crew was in tearing high spirits the day Georgie's secret came out. It was a beautiful day, and the *Jupiter* was anchored near shore. While some of the crew went ashore to find fresh water, others doffed their clothes and jumped in the sea for a swim.

It embarrassed Georgie to be around so many naked men, even after a year with the Karankawas. So she retired to Lafitte's quarters and looked for something to read. He had a great many books, but most were in French or Spanish — languages she didn't know. However, she did manage to find a volume of poetry written in English. She had just settled down to peruse it when Bronson bounded into the room radiating his usual high spirits.

"C'mon, Georgie Boy! Put the bloody book down and come for a swim!"

"No thanks, Bron. I'd rather stay here," she said.

"Nonsense! No one with any sense would rather read than swim on a day like this."

"Well I do," said Georgie, getting a bit testy.

The Irishman laughed. "That's no way to talk to your elders, boy-o. You're goin'."

And with that, Bronson picked her up, slung her over his shoulder like a sack of meal, and carried her to the deck.

"Bronson, no! Put me down!" she said. A note of hysteria had crept into her voice, but he either didn't notice or didn't care.

"Right you are," he said, dumping her on the deck. "Now off with your clothes!"

He stripped off his linen shirt and reached for her.

"Bronson, no!" she cried. "No! I'm a girl!"

Silence. Nothing made a sound except the water against *Jupiter*'s hull. Several of the men snatched up clothing to cover their privates. Georgie would have laughed if she hadn't been so scared.

"Great Saint Brigid, the boy's serious. He's a girl!" said Bronson. "What have you gone and done to yourself, Georgie?!"

CHAPTER 19

The crew didn't like it — not one bit. Women were bad luck on a pirate ship.

"I understand why you did it," Lafitte told her that night. "I just wish you could have kept your secret another week or so. We're going home with the hold only half full."

His men were positively mutinous. To calm them, he'd had to turn the ship for home. They would rather forego booty than sail with a girl on board.

When she apologized for the sixth time, he made a dismissive gesture with his hand.

"Never mind," he said. "It will be good to spend a few days at home. Besides, you'll be good company for Jeanette."

"Who's Jeanette?" she asked.

"My daughter."

When she asked for more details, he would only say she'd have plenty of time to get to know the girl.

Once he got over the shock, Bronson thought it a great joke that Georgie was a girl. He told the story of Georgie's revelation again and again, even though most everyone had been there when it happened. No one thought it as funny as he did.

Two days after they started for home, Bronson called her on deck.

"We're here," he said. "Come see."

She went eagerly, anxious to see this great town the men spoke of with so much enthusiasm. But when she looked where Bron pointed, all she saw was a long, sandy barrier island at the mouth of a bay. It looked like any one of the Karankawas' summer campsites. From this distance, the clustered buildings even looked like ba-aks.

As they got closer, she saw that she wasn't all that far off. Most of the buildings seemed to be made of bits of sail and old timbers. Some looked very much like the shelter she'd built herself when she first washed up on these shores.

But there were two exceptions. They sat on slightly higher ground than the other buildings, and one seemed to glow red in the afternoon sun. When she asked Bronson about them, he nodded. "Aye, that's the fort and Lafitte's own house, La Maison Rouge. That's French for The Red House," he whispered.

When they finally landed, a great many people were waiting for them, including one beautiful dark-haired girl.

"Papa!" she cried, as Lafitte stepped ashore.

"Jeanette, mon cher. Look what I have brought you," he said, motioning for Georgie to step forward.

"What?" said the girl, looking eagerly past Georgie. "What did you bring me?"

"This! I brought you a playmate," he said, laying a hand on Georgie's shoulder.

Georgie didn't like the feeling that she was a piece of property — something to be disposed of at Lafitte's whim. He seemed to have forgotten that it was *she* who saved eight of *his* men. Surely that counted for something.

Apparently not, because a moment later, Jeanette looked her up and down and heaved a great sigh.

"Oh, all right then. Come on," she said to Georgie.

Georgie looked at Lafitte, but he was deep in conversation with a man Georgie had never seen before. Bronson was nowhere to be found. It seemed she had no choice. She followed the sulky girl up a muddy street toward La Maison Rouge.

CHAPTER 20

Campeachy was much bigger than it had seemed from the deck of the *Jupiter*. In addition to the fort and Lafitte's house, it boasted docks, an arsenal, and a shipyard.

It had one long dirt street that turned muddy whenever it rained. On each side of that street were houses and shops, including a boardinghouse and several gambling rooms. People from all over the world visited the town to buy the goods Lafitte and his men stole from Spain. Bronson said almost two thousand people called Campeachy home.

For the time being, Georgie was one of them. By the time summer arrived, she knew the town quite well. She knew Jeanette pretty well too and often thought to herself that she liked the town better. Much better.

Jeanette viewed Georgie as her own personal servant and called her "Girl." Georgie hated that. It made her feel like one of the poor Africans who were bought and sold at Campeachy's slave market. She hated that place and avoided it whenever possible. She was convinced the air shimmered with the fear and anger of those being sold. And the piteous cries of mothers and children who were separated and sold to different masters gave her nightmares.

She loved the docks and went there as often as she could. She liked talking with visitors and always asked them about the *Mary Maud* and her family. So far no one had known a thing about the ill-fated ship. But she refused to give up hope. Jeanette insisted that her parents must be dead, but Georgie clung to the belief that they weren't. Some days it was the only thing that kept her going.

Georgie lived at La Maison Rouge. It was a beautiful house with two towers, each with a cannon mounted on top that faced out to sea. When Lafitte was home, Georgie had her own bedroom and ate with the family. But when he was gone, Jeanette made her eat with the servants and sleep in the cellar. Georgie didn't mind — she liked the servants, and it was much cooler in the cellar than anyplace else in the house. But she was careful not to let Jeanette know that.

Bronson had his own house but was a frequent visitor to La Maison Rouge. He always brought Georgie a present when he did — something that aggravated Jeanette to no end, since he didn't bring presents to her. Georgie suspected that Bronson knew how Jeanette felt — and how she treated Georgie — because he always waited to give Georgie her gift until the other girl was out of the room. That only made her love Bronson more. The better she got to know him, the more he reminded her of Jeff.

He wasn't around much, though. Lafitte kept him busy with the fleet. She'd finally learned to say "privateer" instead of "pirate." Lafitte was in Campeachy more often than his mate. He was the one and only law in town, and if he wasn't there, disputes didn't get settled and criminals didn't get prosecuted. He administered two main punishments — whipping and hanging. Murder, robbery, mutiny, and stealing from Lafitte's ships were all hanging offenses. And when Lafitte hanged someone, he let the body dangle from the gallows for days as a warning to others. That horrified Georgie. Even after all these months, she hadn't gotten used to the sight — not to mention the smell! — of a decaying body swaying in the summer breezes.

There was something odd about Lafitte, something she simply couldn't figure out. He was barbaric in so many ways. Yet he insisted on the finest furnishings and table settings for his house. He served wine imported from France and had hired a cook from New Orleans. He loved to entertain, and when he did, Jeanette and Georgie were expected to dress up and act like ladies.

This was the one thing she and Jeanette agreed on — they hated all those long, tedious dinners with Lafitte's stuffy business associates. Among his most frequent guests that summer were two slave traders from Louisiana, Jim and Rezin Bowie. The brothers bragged on and on about how much money they had made smuggling Africans into Louisiana. Georgie thought this was revolting. Jeanette just found them boring.

Despite their different motives, Georgie and Jeanette cooperated to make the Bowies as uncomfortable as they were during those dinners. Early in the day Georgie would distract the cook so Jeanette could sneak into the kitchen and steal pinches of hot pepper powder and bitter herbs. Then they added the spices to the Bowies' food under the guise of passing platters back and forth to one another. The brothers never dared say a word for fear of insulting Lafitte.

CHAPTER 21

One particularly hot day, near the end of summer, Georgie escaped up one of La Maison Rouge's towers. It was the perfect place to take advantage of the gusty breeze blowing off the ocean. She was facing into the wind with her eyes half closed when a movement out at sea caught her attention. It was the *Jupiter*, home early and racing into port. Lafitte's flagship was the fastest craft in the Gulf of Mexico. When she moved like that, it was because someone was in a hurry. Georgie knew that something must be wrong, and she headed for the docks. At least five hundred people had already gathered there. They'd all seen the *Jupiter*'s unexpected return.

"Storm's coming," said Bronson as he stepped ashore with Lafitte. "A bad one. We raced it back, but we didn't beat it by much."

He and Lafitte split up and started giving orders.

"Georgie, gather all the women and children and get them to Maison Rouge," Lafitte said. "Hurry! Go now."

Georgie was disappointed. She'd been sure the Spainards were after the *Jupiter*, and she'd been hoping to see the tower cannons fired. But a storm — that's what all the fuss was about? Georgie shook her head. How bad could it be? But there was no one to ask. Everybody was rushing around following orders, so Georgie followed suit and began rounding up the women. Many of them insisted on packing a few belongings to take with them, so it took several hours to get to them all. By the time they were crowded into La Maison Rouge, the wind was howling and the sky was an ominous black tinged with green. The sea looked angry.

There was no more room in the house, so Lafitte and Bronson decided to try to ride out the storm in the *Jupiter*. Jeanette wanted to go with them, but her father insisted she stay at La Maison Rouge. It sat on the island's highest point of land.

"You'll be safest there," he told her.

First the hail fell. Bappity, bappity, bappity. Then came the rain. The wind howled and clawed at the shutters like an animal trying to get at its prey. The women wept and prayed as the hurricane raged throughout the night.

Georgie moved from room to room, offering what comfort she could — food, a sip of water, a hug, or a prayer. To her surprise, Jeanette did the same. Just before dawn the pirate's daughter offered to take a tea tray upstairs while Georgie helped the cook make breakfast. She had been gone only a few minutes when a mighty crash shook the house and screams came tumbling down the stairs. Georgie dashed to see what had happened and froze when she reached the second floor. The roof of the west tower had collapsed under the weight of its cannon, crushing the women sheltering in the room below.

"Jeanette!" called Georgie. "Jeanette!"

She heard a moan in the far corner and carefully picked her way through the debris to find the person making the sound. It was Martha Graham, the gunsmith's wife. Her leg stuck out at an odd angle from her body, obviously broken in several places.

"Hold on, Martha. We'll get the doctor here for you," said Georgie.

The woman nodded and pointed at something directly behind Georgie, who whirled to see what it was. The cannon was there, on its side. And peeking from beneath it was the end of a lovely purple silk shawl that had come all the way from Paris, France. It was one of Jeanette's favorites.

· • ■ ☠ ■ • ·

CHAPTER 22

Georgie had thought the worst thing she could ever go through was the sinking of the *Mary Maud*. But she'd been wrong. The sun dawned that morning on a world she barely recognized.

The island was ravaged.

Standing on the undamaged tower of La Maison Rouge, Georgie saw water where land had been and shattered timbers where houses used to be. And the bodies — they were strewn everywhere. It was impossible for her to look in any direction without seeing hundreds of broken bodies — the bodies of people she knew.

Only three ships had escaped the hurricane's fury — the *Jupiter*, the *Pride*, and the *Gustav*. Lafitte's face was tight and expressionless when he was told what happened to Jeanette and the others. But when Georgie passed his room at night, she heard him sobbing.

She said nothing to Lafitte for fear of embarrassing him, but she did tell Bronson. She hoped he could help somehow. But he didn't know what to do for Lafitte either.

"The captain feels guilty because he made her stay at the house, I'll wager. It's not his fault, what happened, but I imagine he thinks it is," Bronson said.

The pirate channeled his grief into rebuilding the colony. First he divided the survivors into groups and set different tasks for them. Some cleared debris, while others rebuilt houses. The unlucky ones were assigned to bury the dead.

Georgie volunteered to search the island for anything the colonists could eat. Because of her year with the Karankawa, she knew what to look for. Bronson did not like sending her on such a dangerous mission. Bands of Karankawa were known to cross over from the mainland from time to time. Lafitte's men had had trouble with them in the past. But the colony's situation was precarious, so he let her do it. He assigned six women to help her and sent along two of his men armed with rifles and plenty of shot.

They brought back berries and roots, seeds, turtles, and fish. Georgie even overcame her squeamishness and snared several birds.

But her greatest find was the oyster bed. She'd promised herself she would never eat another oyster, but that seemed silly in light of the current situation. So she led her helpers along the coast, looking for a likely spot, and found it about halfway down the island.

Nearby, out of the range of the firesticks, a pair of dark eyes watched as Georgie splashed in the shallow water, laughing as she and the others filled baskets with the mussels.

· • ■ ☠ ■ • ·

CHAPTER 23

Winter was coming, and even with the food that Georgie and her group provided, the colony still faced starvation. The situation was critical.

Eleven days after the storm, Georgie heard Lafitte and Bronson arguing in the pirate's study.

"You can't do this, Captain. It isn't right," said Bronson. "The men will never stand for it."

She didn't hear Lafitte's reply, but Bronson stomped out soon after. He didn't even tell her goodbye. The next day she found out why he was so angry. Lafitte called the survivors together on the docks and told them there was not enough food for everyone.

"Nor do we have the money to buy additional supplies," he said. "Therefore, I leave today for New Orleans," he said. "And with me will go every African now on the island."

Low murmurs soon turned to screams and angry shouts as the news sank in. There could be only one reason for Lafitte's actions: He intended to sell the island's black population in the slave markets of New Orleans. Bronson stood by Lafitte stony-faced as the sailors who had married African women protested.

Lafitte's face turned ugly. "This is not a democracy! I make the rules here and I have spoken. We sail with the tide."

No one dared to argue. In Lafitte's present state of mind, arguments would be considered mutiny. And in Campeachy, mutiny was punished with death. A few of the island's black residents managed to escape, but the majority were loaded into the hold of the *Jupiter* and sold outright or traded for things like coffee and flour. Georgie wouldn't touch the stuff, and it was months before she could bring herself to eat anything she hadn't picked or caught herself.

Lafitte had returned to a sullen colony and a surprise visitor.

The United States had sent a fellow named Colonel George Graham with an ultimatum for Lafitte. He was to stop his privateering in the Gulf or face the wrath of the United States Navy. Lafitte charmed the colonel, agreed to his terms, and swore allegiance once again to the United States. The only one he fooled was Colonel Graham.

· • ■ ☠ ■ • ·

CHAPTER 24

The winter passed without further incident, and to the surprise of no one who lived in Campeachy, Lafitte made no attempt to curtail his piratical ways in the Gulf or leave the island.

By the time spring arrived, the colony had been largely rebuilt and was beginning to thrive again.

Georgie saw a butterfly from the window of La Maison Rouge one day and smiled. She liked to think of them as good omens, kisses from Mother Nature. Swift on the heels of that thought was the realization that another whole year had passed since the *Mary Maud* went down. She was twelve now. Jeff would be thirteen — if he was still alive.

Tears welled up and escaped from her eyes in spite of her best efforts to keep them in. She found that she talked about her family less and less but thought about them more than ever.

"Why the long face?" asked Bronson.

When she told him, he nodded sympathetically. Bronson almost always did.

"Bron, I don't think I can stay here much longer. I have to find out if my family is out there."

"I know, dearie, but you can't go on your own," he said. "Try to bide your time. Everything happens for a reason."

Georgie knew he was trying to comfort her, but the only thing she felt was irritation.

Whenever she broached the subject with Lafitte, he always had an excuse for why she couldn't go and why he couldn't take her. With Jeanette gone, he relied upon her more than ever with his guests, he said. Any mention of Jeanette made Georgie feel guilty and she would drop the subject — for a few months at least. She began to suspect he did that on purpose. He never mentioned his daughter at any other time.

One day Lafitte summoned her and told her to put on her prettiest dress.

"We're having a very special guest for dinner tonight — at least he thinks he's very important!" Lafitte chuckled at his own witticism but would tell Georgie nothing else about the guest.

As it turned out, the fellow's name was James Long. He was a doctor from Mississippi, and Georgie disliked him at once. There was something sneaky about Long that made her reluctant to turn her back on him. And he was so full of himself and his grandiose plans for an independent Republic of Texas — with him as its leader, of course — that he couldn't tell Lafitte was mocking him. He even offered to make Lafitte the admiral of the Texas navy.

When Georgie told Lafitte how she felt, he laughed.

"You are sharp, Miss Georgina, a fine judge of character. He's ambitious, that one. It will be the making or the death of him. That is certain."

More and more, Lafitte reminded Georgie of a fox — sly and secretive, always alert for trouble and often causing it.

Many months after Long's visit to La Maison Rouge, word reached Campeachy that Long's men had been intercepted and attacked by soldiers from Spain, who killed many, jailed others, and scattered the rest. Long himself had fled back to Mississippi. This was a juicy bit of news in Campeachy — to everyone except Lafitte, who seemed not the least bit surprised.

CHAPTER 25

· • ■ ☠ ■ • ·

Ulanga sighed. She had a bad feeling about this, but Tunkutu would not listen to her. None of them would. They thought Gor-gee was being held by the Pale Smelly Ones against her will and were determined to rescue her.

There was no way Ulanga could convince them otherwise without admitting that she had helped the girl escape.

At first it had seemed that her plan worked. Gor-gee had warned the foreigners and fled with them before the warriors could attack. The men had been furious, but none had been killed in a foolish charge against enemies with firesticks.

Tunkutu had spent weeks searching the coastline, hoping the foreigners would land again. It was a matter of pride with him; they had stolen one of his family members. But as time passed, his anger had lessened. Gor-gee was rarely mentioned in camp anymore.

Then Rohana had returned from a hunting expedition to Snake Island. He had seen Gor-gee there, gathering oysters. He said two Pale Ones used firesticks to make her work for them.

The news sent the camp into an uproar. No longer was Gor-gee the strange foreign child who had lived with them for a short time. To hear the men talk, she was a prized maiden of the People stolen by the Pale Ones. They would avenge her honor. They would get her back. They would not be denied their fight a second time.

The entire camp had packed up and made the long trip to an area near Snake Island. The women were to stay on the mainland while the men crossed over and liberated Gor-gee. Ulanga had never felt so helpless.

CHAPTER 26

Georgie stooped to pick up an acorn and quickly snapped it toward Bronson's head. Direct hit! She laughed as he turned to see who had launched the little missile.

He smiled, but not for long. "No more fooling around, Georgie. Let's get this done," he said.

"Bron, you're turning into an old woman. Relax for heaven's sake," said Georgie.

She had finally convinced Lafitte to let her out of town to visit the oyster beds again and collect some berries, and she intended to enjoy herself. Campeachy was wearing on her. But Bron was determined to be a stick-in-the-mud. He'd insisted that four armed men accompany Georgie and the two women helping her because some Karankawas had visited the island several weeks ago. Four guards and three workers! She thought it was ridiculous and told him so.

Up ahead she saw a stand of three great oak trees and pleaded with him to let them stop there for lunch.

"Okay, Georgie, but on one condition only," he said.

What that condition was to have been, Georgie never knew. As Bronson opened his mouth to speak, his body jerked and blood poured from his chest as an arrow found its mark.

"Kronks! Kronks!" cried the other guards, as Bronson collapsed in front of Georgie.

She ran to him as shots rang out and war cries pierced the air. Dropping to her knees, she put her hands over the wound to try and stop the bleeding. Bronson made a gurgling sound as he tried to speak, and Georgie looked up just in time to see the light fade from his eyes.

"Bronson, no!" she screamed.

Georgie felt a tremendous blow on her right side and toppled over onto Bronson. She tried to stand but couldn't seem to move. She was dizzy, and darkness seemed to be creeping in from both sides. Seconds before she slid into unconsciousness, a face loomed into her line of vision.

"Tunkutu!" she said. Then the darkness took her.

Chapter 27

· • ∞ ✄ ♋ • ·

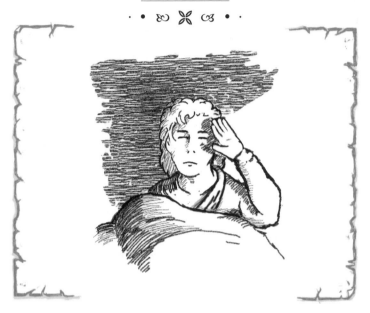

"**A**re you awake?"

Georgie groaned and tried to shield her eyes from the light.

"Come on now, sit up. I've brought your breakfast," said Cook.

"I'm not hungry," said Georgie. "Please, take it away."

It had been three weeks since the battle at Three Trees. Georgie's shoulder, which was hit by a stray bullet, was mending. Her spirits were not. Bronson was dead. Two of the other men and one of the women who'd been with her were dead, too. She'd been told two Karankawa warriors had been killed and several wounded. One of the dead Indians had been described to her as "a mighty big fella, even for a Kronk."

And here she sat, her arm in a sling. Tears welled in her eyes again. Why did I survive? She'd asked herself that question at least twice a day since waking up back at La Maison Rouge. Why did I survive the shipwreck? Why did I survive the battle?

A knock on the door pulled her from her musings.

"Georgie?" called Lafitte. "Can I come in?"

Georgie didn't answer. He knocked again. "Georgie, there's someone here to see you."

As the door creaked open, Georgie grabbed a pillow from behind her head and tossed it toward the doorway with her good arm and pulled the covers over her head. Her visitor chuckled.

"You missed," said a familiar voice. "C'mon, Georgie, you can do better than that!"

As Georgie poked her head out of the covers, her eyes widened at the sight of a tall young man with sandy hair and blue eyes.

"Jeff?"

Behind him hovered two more familiar faces.

"Mother?" she said in wonderment. "Father?"

Lafitte ushered them into the room, a big smile on his face. "Guess what?" he said. "I finally tracked down the *Mary Maud.*"

Epilogue, 1821

It turned out that quite a few people had survived the shipwreck. Jeff and her parents had managed to stay aboard the *Mary Maud* until the boat was finally grounded on a sandbar on the Louisiana coast. Instead of going on to Mississippi, they stayed there, hoping to get news of Georgie. Everyone told them she must surely be dead, but they always held out hope. And when Lafitte's message finally reached them, they packed up everything they owned and headed for Texas. In the two years since they'd been reunited, they had lived in Campeachy and prospered. But now the United States had forced Lafitte to leave his colony. Before leaving, he tore down the fort, scuttled all but three of his ships, and set fire to what was left of the town. There were already rumors that he'd left treasure behind on the island.

Georgie stood with her family on the deck of the U.S. warship *Enterprise*, watching the fire reflected in Galveston Bay. At times the flames looked like bright fingers on the dark water, reaching out to Lafitte's ships, which grew smaller and smaller until, at long last, they slipped over the horizon and disappeared into the Gulf.

The American captain approached her father. "What will you do now, sir?"

"Well, we never did make it to Mississippi," he said. "We could try that. But I hear there's a fellow named Austin starting a colony here in Texas. I'm thinking of joining him."

He turned to his daughter.

"Georgie, you've spent more time here than any of us. Would you like that?"

She considered the idea a moment and then smiled.

"I think that would be wonderful," she said. "As long as we're together."

The End

THE REAL STORY

The Karankawa Indians

In *Marooned on the Pirate Coast*, Georgie lives for more than a year with Native Americans that we call the Karankawas. Like many indigenous people, they called themselves People or Human Beings. They were one of several tribes that lived on the Texas coast before European and American settlers moved in. According to many accounts, they were fierce cannibals!

If you believe some historic tales, the Karankawas roasted victims alive and munched on human flesh in the same way that people living in Texas today would chow down on Chee-tos or Hershey bars. But the truth — what we know of it anyway — paints quite a different picture. While the Karankawas undoubtedly did practice ritual cannibalism — that is, they sometimes did eat humans on special occasions — they mostly ate fish, oysters, deer, clams, berries, fruit, and other things that they could catch or find on the wild shores of Texas. When they did eat people, it was probably a way of insulting an enemy and taking his strength.

The real Karankawas looked and lived as they do in *Marooned on the Pirate Coast*. They lived in ba-aks, adored their children, and had customs like the crying rituals and mitotes. They didn't have chiefs like other tribes, but they did have medicine men. One ritual in *Marooned on the Pirate Coast* is completely fictional — Georgie's adoption ceremony. Everything else in the story is true or based on what we know the Karankawas really did.

Karankawa men often grew to be six feet tall or even bigger. That isn't so unusual today, but it was back then. During those times, most of the Europeans and Americans were much shorter, and the size of the Karankawa men impressed them. Karankawa braves usually went naked but decorated their bodies with tattoos and paint. They pierced their lips and even their chests with pieces of cane. Ouch! The women pierced their lips, too, and sometimes were tattooed. Unmarried girls often wore a black stripe down the middle of their faces, just like Georgie does. The hair of the Karankawas was often described as cinnamon-colored because it had a reddish hue.

The men hunted with bows that were as tall as they were and made of cedar. Even the arrows were big — up to three feet long — and could pierce right through an animal or enemy. The men prized their bows and took very good care of them. And they were also very skilled with them. They even fished with bows and arrows instead of nets or poles.

The women wore pabigos, skirts made of moss or skins, and were in charge of making camp and gathering foods like oysters, berries, and other plants. Sometimes they hunted small animals like rabbits and turtles. They made pottery and probably made baskets, and they collected asphaltum — naturally occurring tar balls that washed up on shore — to waterproof the pottery. Sometimes the men even chewed the tar balls like we chew gum today. Some people think that the tar on Galveston's beaches is from pollution, but it's not.

Life was very harsh for the Karankawas, and they rarely had enough to eat. They moved from place to place, always in search of food.

The Karankawas were quite different from other Native American tribes in Texas — Plains Indians, such as the Apache or Comanche, and mound builders like the Caddo. They were probably descended from people who lived on islands in the Caribbean Sea. They might have ended up in Texas on purpose, seeking a new life like the Americans and Europeans who would follow them. Or, like Georgie in *Marooned on the Pirate Coast*, they might have simply been blown off course in a storm and deposited on the Texas shore where they made the best of things.

Much of what we know about the Karankawas comes from Alvar Nunez Cabeza de Vaca, a Spanish explorer who was one of only a few survivors of a shipwreck on the Texas coast in 1528. He lived among the Karankawas for more than four years as a slave, medicine man, and trader before finally escaping to Mexico.

Almost three hundred years passed before significant numbers of white settlers began moving into Karankawa territory. In real life, relations between the settlers and the Karankawas were just like they are in *Marooned on the Pirate Coast* — bad. The settlers stole from the natives, and the natives stole from the settlers. The settlers killed the Indians, and the Indians killed the settlers — you get the idea. Neither understood the other, trusted the other, or, for the most part, liked the other. Of course, the Karankawas didn't get along with other Indians, either. Not even other groups of Karankawas. They were very unfriendly to outsiders, with a few exceptions like Cabeza de Vaca.

These days, all that remains of the Karankawas is the stories about them and their name on places like Carancahua (another spelling for Karankawa) Point in Galveston Bay. They were hunted and driven out by the American and European settlers. The last living members of the tribe migrated to Mexico and intermarried with the natives there. They were probably extinct by 1847.

Jean Lafitte and Galveston Island

It's hard to separate fact from fiction when you're talking about Jean Lafitte. He's been called pirate, businessman, patriot, spy and scoundrel, charming and ruthless. One thing we do know for certain — Texas was one of the last stops in his long and interesting life.

At least half a dozen places in three countries, including Westchester in New York State, have been touted as his birthplace. But most people think he was born in Bayonne, France, sometime in 1780 or 1781.

"Jean Lafitte" from *A History of Texas*, by Louis J. Wortham, 1924. Courtesy of Texas State Library and Archives Commission.

He and his brother Pierre settled in New Orleans sometime between 1804 and 1808, and from there they ran many profitable businesses, including profiteering. That is, piracy.

By most accounts, he was charming and handsome, at least when he was young. By the time he left Galveston, people reported he looked ill, overweight, and tired.

He fought for the United States during the War of 1812, and because of that, the U.S. president pardoned him and his brother for their swashbuckling ways. But they went right back to it, much to the annoyance of the United States government.

In 1817 the Lafittes took over another pirate's camp on Galveston Island and named it Campeachy (sometimes spelled Campeche). Life there was just as it is depicted in *Marooned on the Pirate Coast.* He built a fort and a fabulous house of red-painted stone for himself and imported fine food, wine, and other material goods. Though many denounced him as a blood-thirsty pirate, they were eager to buy the goods he looted from Spanish galleons. Ships from all over the world docked in Galveston Bay to take advantage of the bargains. From Campeachy, Lafitte sold slaves, operated a fleet of pirate ships — he preferred the term "privateer" — and was the absolute, unquestioned ruler. Anyone who disobeyed was punished swiftly and severely. Hangings and beatings were common.

He considered himself a patriot and swore allegiance to the United States but spied for Spain. In the end, he was true only to himself.

The Jeanette in *Marooned on the Pirate Coast* was a real person, but different stories make her out to be Lafitte's daughter, housekeeper, or girlfriend.

In 1821 the United States gave him an ultimatum: Leave Galveston or else. He chose to leave, but not before scuttling most of his fleet and burning the settlement. When he sailed out of Galveston in 1821, he was sailing out of history, too. His death is as mysterious as his birth. But his legend lives on.

Jim Bowie and the Slave Trade in Early Texas

James Bowie is best known as a hero of the Alamo, but he was part of Texas history long before that famous battle. Born in Kentucky in 1796, he grew up in Louisiana. From a base there, he and his brother Rezin began trading slaves after the War of 1812.

Back then, one of the biggest slave markets in the Western Hemisphere was on Galveston Island. Jean Lafitte and his pirates captured the slaves from Spanish ships and sold them cheap. The Bowie brothers bought them, often forty at a time, and smuggled them into Louisiana where they sold them for ten times what they had paid for them. According to some accounts, Jean Lafitte himself sometimes delivered slaves to Jim and Rezin in Louisiana. It didn't take long for the brothers to save a small fortune. When they had earned $65,000, the Bowies retired from the slave trade.

Many years later, on March 6, 1836, Jim Bowie was in the Alamo, sick with a fever, when the Mexican army stormed the fortress and killed him and all its defenders.

James Long

James Long was a doctor who believed Texas should belong to the United States and tried to make that happen long before it did.

He was born in Virginia and lived many places before settling down with his wife on a plantation in Mississippi. Dr. Long had served with Andrew Jackson in the Battle of New Orleans during the War of 1812, so he had experience as a soldier, too. In 1819 he led about one hundred twenty people into Texas, seized the East Texas town of Nacogdoches, and declared Texas independent with himself as president.

Dr. Long wanted Jean Lafitte's help, and just as he did in *Marooned on the Pirate Coast*, the doctor tried to entice the pirate to join his scheme as admiral of the Texas navy. But Lafitte betrayed him to the Spanish government, and Long was forced to flee for his life.

He returned to the United States, but he was not done with Texas. Not quite. In 1820 he returned to Texas, this time to the Bolivar Peninsula near Galveston. He left his pregnant wife, Jane, at a poorly provisioned fort there while he and about fifty others went to join the fight at a place called La Bahia. His wife never saw him again. He was caught and sent to Mexico where he died in a mysterious shooting in 1822. Some say it was accidental, but others claim that the so-called accident was arranged.

Hurricanes and Galveston Island

Galveston is famous for the hurricane in September 1900 that killed six to eight thousand people and caused about forty million dollars in property damage. Even today, it's considered the worst natural disaster in United States history. But it wasn't the only hurricane to strike the island.

One hit in 1776, but few people were there to see it.

The storm depicted in *Marooned on the Pirate Coast* really did happen in 1818. Jean Lafitte rode it out on his ship, leaving his house on the high ground to the town's womenfolk. Unfortunately, he hadn't counted on a cannon crashing through the roof. Many of the women he'd tried to protect died and some were maimed. The fort collapsed and most of the ships and houses on the island were destroyed. As many as a thousand people died.

All the houses on Galveston Island were destroyed again in 1837 thanks to "Racer's Storm," a terrible wind that caused damage from the Yucatan Peninsula to South Carolina.

In 1842 a hurricane caused at least fifty thousand dollars worth of damage there, but no one died.

Galveston was flooded again and sustained damage totaling about one million dollars when a hurricane raked the entire Texas coast in 1867.

Forty-eight years later, 275 people died during a storm that lasted three days in August of 1915 and caused fifty million dollars worth of damage.

Another great storm struck near Galveston in 1943.

The largest hurricane on record in Texas happened in September of 1961. Hurricane Carla spawned a tornado that wrecked Galveston and caused damage up and down the Texas coast that cost more than three hundred million dollars. Thirty-four people died, and four hundred sixty-five were injured.

In 1983 Hurricane Alicia spun off thirty-two tornados and struck hardest at Galveston and Houston, killing eighteen people and causing about three billion dollars in damage. Another eighteen hundred people were hurt.

And in 1989 yet another storm washed ashore, affecting Harris, Galveston, and Brazoria Counties.

It's inevitable that Galveston will continue to be plagued by hurricanes, but thanks to modern technology and well-planned evacuation routes, people are no longer at their mercy.

Three Trees

One of Galveston's earliest and most enduring landmarks is a grove of oak trees — guess how many? — near the center of the island. The Karankawa natives often camped there or used it as a neutral meeting place. The Indians battled Jean Lafitte and his men at the grove in 1817 after some of the pirates kidnapped a Karankawa maiden — an event that inspired part of Georgie's story in *Marooned on the Pirate Coast.* In 1821, after Lafitte left Galveston for good, treasure seekers speculated that the pirate had buried some of his booty in the grove. When they arrived at Three Trees to find Karankawas already camped there and celebrating, they attacked the Indians.

Legend has it that shortly before leaving Galveston (which the Karankawas called Snake Island), Lafitte was overheard saying he'd "buried his treasure under the three trees." But when some of his men dug up a box there, it contained the body of a woman. Precious to Lafitte, perhaps, but useless to treasure hunters. Today tourists tramp all over Galveston looking for the famous trees. Oak trees can live hundreds of years, so it's possible that the originals are still alive. One grove of more than a dozen trees, some of them very old, has a marker identifying it as "Lafitte's Grove." Find Three Trees, and you can take a rest under the very same branches that once offered shade to generations of Texans, including the Karankawas and Jean Lafitte.

Sources

Bedichek, Roy. *Karankaway Country*. Austin: University of Texas Press, 1989.

Bollarrt, William. "Life of Jean Lafitte." *United Service Magazine*, October-November 1851.

Calvert, Robert A. and Arnoldo De Leon. *The History of Texas*. Wheeling, Illinois: Harlan Davidson, Inc., 1996.

Cartwright, Gary. *Galveston: A History of the Island*. Fort Worth: TCU Press, 1991.

Fehrenbach, T. R. *Lone Star: A History of Texas and Texans*. New York: Da Capo Press, 2000.

Gonzalez, Catherine Troxell. *Lafitte: The Terror of the Gulf*. Austin: Eakin Press, 1981.

Grun, Bernard. *The Timetables of History: A Horizontal Linkage of People and Events*. New York: Simon and Schuster, Inc., 1982.

Haley, James L. *Texas: From the Frontier to Spindletop*. New York: St. Martin's Press, 1985.

McComb, David G. *Texas: A Modern History*. Austin: University of Texas Press, 1989.

Newcomb, W.W. Jr. *The Indians of Texas: From Prehistoric to Modern Times*. Austin: University of Texas Press, 1995.

Ramsay, Jack C. Jr. *Jean Laffite: Prince of Pirates*. Austin: Eakin Press, 1996.

Saxon, Lyle. *Lafitte the Pirate*. New Orleans: Borman House, 1948.

Spears, John B. "Lafitte, the Last of the Buccaneers." *Outing Magazine*, May 1911, p. 242.

Also

The Handbook of Texas Online

Quarterly of the Texas State Historical Association